W9-CMM-951

CONTENTS

A GIRL CALLED BOY

A GIRL CALLED BOY

Belinda Hurmence

CLARION BOOKS
New York

CURR
PZ
7
.H9567
G.
1982

CLARION BOOKS
a Houghton Mifflin Company imprint
215 Park Avenue South, New York, NY 10003

Library of Congress Cataloging in Publication Data
Hurmence, Belinda. A girl called Boy.
SUMMARY: A pampered young black girl who has been
mysteriously transported back to the days of slavery,
struggles to escape her bondage.
[1. Space and time—Fiction. 2. Slavery in the
United States—Fiction] I. Title.
PZ7.H9567Gi   [Fic]   80-28066
PA ISBN 0-395-55698-8   ISBN 0-395-31022-9   AACR1

AGM 10 9

for Howard

-1-

BELLEMONT OVERLOOK

A skinny but fine-framed young girl with close-cropped hair poked a stick at the smoldering charcoal.

Her mother said, "I wish you'd leave the fire alone, Boy."

In the humidity, the charcoal had been slow to ignite, and Boy's mother knew that stirring it around would only delay the bed of coals they needed for cooking. "Why don't you bring the picnic baskets down from the car?"

"Let LeMont do it," said the girl. "You never make him do anything." At her age, eleven, that was the way she often answered her mother, with the suggestion of a pout.

Her father said, "Stop messing with the fire, Boy. Didn't you hear what your mother said?"

On that sultry August day, in the mountains of western North Carolina, two black families, the Yanceys and the Jurnigans, had assembled at lunchtime in the Bellemont Overlook picnic area. The adults lounged around a concrete table with potato chips and cans of cold drinks at hand, waiting for the grill fire to burn down to coals.

The girl ignored her father's request as she had ignored her mother's. For Boy Yancey, though basically dutiful, was spoiled in many ways, and clever enough to gauge her parents' indulgence precisely.

Boy was not her real name, of course. Her real name was Overtha, Blanche Overtha Yancey, after her two grandmothers. Around Freetown they mostly called her Boy because of her initials, and she preferred it.

Not that she was a tomboy; she wasn't, although her oldest brother LeMont insisted her summer haircut made her look like a boy. And not that she didn't like being a girl; she did. But Blanche? Ugh. *Overtha?* She loved both her mamaws, but she did wish she had a regular name, like Linda or Susan or Donna. Her parents said the mamaws were named for their grandmothers, and they felt Boy should be too. It was tradition in their family. Tradition, tradition.

When LeMont and Junior Jurnigan emerged from the forest trail to join the party, Boy left off stirring the charcoal and approached the picnic table where the boys displayed their treasures, various colored pebbles from the stream that ran below the picnic area.

Junior turned a dull, grayish-brown rock in his hands. "This looked so neat in the water," he remarked in disappointment.

"Soapstone," Boy's father told him. "It doesn't look like much until it's wet or polished. I've got an old pocket piece here made of African soapstone." He compared a smooth, slender carving with Junior's rough fragment. "Notice how they both have the same soapy feel to them?"

From as far back as Boy could remember, her father had carried the curious object in his pocket to touch from time to time, the way some men jingle keys when they are troubled, or thinking. He called it his good luck charm. When Boy was little she thought it was magic, but she didn't believe in magic anymore, except occasionally when she was desperate. Then sometimes it worked.

The tiny sculpture, three inches long or less, bore mere stumps for legs, wings worn away and beak blunted by years of fondling. Still it was recognizable as a bird.

Junior said, "Hey, man, cool," and LeMont said officiously, "That's the bird that ended the Civil War."

"My great-great-grandfather claimed it did," his father agreed with a smile. "At least he claimed it set him free."

"When are we going to eat?" said Boy loudly. She really hoped Daddy wouldn't start bragging about his ancestors.

"Papaw, when he gave it to me, called it the freedom bird," Mr. Yancey said. "It was a conjure, brought over the water, he said. Those old timers put a lot of faith in conjures."

"I'm hungry," Boy whined.

"Well, it made a link with their home country," her father went on. "It was probably a comfort to that first old African, whoever he was, to carry a magic bird around in his pocket. I sort of feel that way myself."

This was too much for Boy, who was mortified that the Jurnigans, and especially Junior Jurnigan, had to listen to stuff that embarrassed her. "Oh, Daddy, you're not African—you're *American.*" She snatched the stone away from him. "Magic," she sneered. "If it was magic enough to set him free, why didn't he make it conjure him back over the water? He must have been awful stupid."

"He wasn't stupid," Boy's mother objected. "He was just ignorant; most slaves were ignorant back then. But that didn't mean they were stupid. "Besides," she added, "Daddy didn't say *he* believed in conjures; he said the slaves did."

"They deserved to be slaves," Boy said, "the way they let themselves be pushed around and never tried to fight back or anything. I wouldn't stand for it. They couldn't make me be a slave."

"Yes, they could," said her brother. LeMont was thirteen, snotty thirteen.

"They could not! I'd run away from them!"

"They'd catch you," said LeMont, enjoying himself. "There'd be these big old bloodhounds on your trail, and when they caught you, they'd bite and tear you, and you'd be hollering and they'd be barking and growling like crazy—gr-r-r!"

"You shut up! They couldn't catch me. I'd buy me a horse and run away on it."

"It was against the law to run away," said Mr. Jurnigan.

Mrs. Jurnigan said, "Slaves couldn't own a horse, they couldn't even ride a horse, unless their master said they could."

"And they couldn't buy anything," Boy's mother said. "It was illegal for them to go into a store, so they couldn't get food or clothing for themselves."

"They had no money to buy things with, anyway," said Boy's father. "Papaw told me they were rationed their food each week, and they only got one set of clothes a year. One pair of shoes. If those didn't fit, they went without. I never saw my great-grandpa in a pair of shoes, even in the wintertime."

Boy shivered.

"Papaw said they could run around over ground spew

in their bare feet," her father continued. "You know what ground spew is, those bristles of ice coming out of the ground that look like a brush squeezed up—well, those tough old slaves—"

"Those tough old slaves," Boy mimicked. "You act like you're proud of them being slaves!"

"Well, Boy, I'm not ashamed," said her father quietly. "Are you?"

"I don't want to talk about it," she muttered. She flounced away from the table and headed for the trail to the stream.

Her mother called, "Don't leave camp, Boy. We're about ready for lunch."

Her father shouted, "Hey, don't run off with my pocket piece. You might lose it."

Boy thrust the stone in her pocket and answered neither of them. She was disgusted with her parents and wanted them to know it. Saying all that in front of Junior Jurnigan! It was the first trip the Jurnigans had made with her family, and Boy guessed it would probably be their last.

A sponge of pine needles cushioned the trail from the picnic area down to where crystalline water bubbled around a stony bend in the creek. At the trail's end, a flat bank thrust a firm, sandy point into the shallows. On the opposite side, a steep bluff reared abruptly from water's edge. If you forded the shallows and penetrated the tangle of alders growing at its base, you could follow a winding staircase of boulders to the top of the bluff—a stiff climb but worth it, because you came out on the lofty knob known as Bellemont Overlook. It was this observation point that gave the picnic area its name.

Boy pulled off her sneakers and dropped them on the

sandspit. Then, considering, she reached in her pocket for the soapstone carving. She was wearing her oldest, best-loved jeans, patched and repatched after many washings, and all the pockets were frayed except for the one that held her ballpoint pen. She didn't want to chance losing her father's magic charm.

In her palm it perched arrogantly on its nubs of legs. She waved it toward the creek. "Take me over the water," she ordered sarcastically. The hollow sockets of its eyes looked beyond, as if into something around or surrounding her. She didn't believe in magic, she reminded herself. Still, that bird's eyes gave her the creeps. She laid the stone into a sneaker for safekeeping, rolled up her jeans and stepped into the water.

"Yike!" she gasped. North Carolina's mountain streams run cold even in midsummer, but this water was icy, icy. It gave her an off-balance feeling besides that came not only from the cold. She felt transfixed, as though she had experienced this water—no, this *moment*—at some time or in some life before; and it seemed to her that queerly from in the air above her own head she looked down and watched herself, standing on one leg in the isolated moment she had experienced before. She shivered, shook her head vigorously and splashed on across the shallows.

The alders grew thicker than she remembered them from last year. She ripped her faded workshirt trying to force her way into the mass, and cat's-claw and horsebrier tore into her bare flesh. Peering into the thicket, she could not discover the familiar cleft rock that marked the beginning of the winding staircase. Also, she had rammed into a broken branch that raked her cheek, and she had to keep swabbing blood with her shirttail.

She gave up and decided to go back to camp. It was time for lunch, anyhow. Then she spied another way up. Downstream, the trunk of an uprooted tree that had fallen in some wet season angled behind the alders from water's edge to the top of the bluff, and the lattice of its branches formed a convenient ladder to the summit. Five minutes later she stood on Bellemont Overlook.

"Down there is Yancey country." (Her father always made this boring speech standing on Bellemont Overlook. Another tradition.) "My people came from this valley, on the other side of the lake."

Bellemont Lake looked different this year, more visible. Other summers it had appeared an interrupted shimmer glimpsed among distant trees.

Daddy's people weren't Yanceys back then, of course, just Bill or John or Mary or whatever. Only after they got their freedom were they allowed last names, usually those of their former masters.

The valley lay somber and gray, very different from summers past, and the leaden sky looked like snow. Boy wished it would snow. What an adventure, picnicking while the flakes drifted down! A freak August snowstorm is unusual in the Smokies, but not unknown in the higher elevations.

Except for the green of pines that mottled the mountainside, the forests stood barren. There must have been a fire, Boy thought. Still, their trunks were not blackened; they just looked dormant, like trees in winter. No wonder the lake showed up so plainly—there weren't many leaves to obscure it.

Looking more closely, she saw a tiny farmhouse in a clearing at the far end of the lake, and at the neck of the valley where the river entered, a tall, gaunt, weathered building. An imposing brick structure with white columns in front dominated the mountain that rose across the lake. These buildings scattered through the valley puzzled Boy, for she had never noticed them before. This was public land, and all the private dwellings, her father said, had been razed long ago when the Park Service acquired it. Perhaps after all these years the Yanceys had come back to their ancestral valley.

There were a lot of Yanceys living in their town, Freetown—black Yanceys as well as white, descendants, doubtless, of this valley's settlers. Now as she contemplated the lonely outposts in the wilderness spread before her, the same eerie aura she had sensed minutes before engulfed her. Gooseflesh prickled her bare arms. She felt cold, and she rolled down the sleeves of her workshirt. Suppose freedom was a trick; suppose in that brick mansion overlooking the lake Yanceys lived again, attended by their slaves?

She turned and scrambled back down the bluff, suddenly in a hurry to get back with her family. The frigid water of the shallows shocked her once again, and for a frozen instant she thought she saw ground spew bristling the shoal on the other side. The illusion vanished like a mirage when she stepped onto the firm sand.

Not only was the ground spew gone; her sneakers had vanished too. How could that be? Sneakers were not a mirage. She knew she wasn't mistaken. She had left them right here on this spot, and she had carefully placed the conjure bird inside one of them for safekeeping.

LeMont, she thought. LeMont had swiped her sneakers. Mama and Daddy let her rotten brother get away with stuff like that all the time. She raced along the pine-needle trail toward camp, filled to the brim with rage and blame.

The trail to the picnic area wound past heavy clumps of laurel and doubled back where sawed stumps of trees opened a track wide enough for a car. The way divided into a rutted twin track and the twin track became almost a crowned road; and the road ran past an old log cabin where the picnic area should have been.

Boy stared at the cabin open-mouthed. How did that get there? How had she missed camp? There was only one trail leading up from the stream that she knew of. She ran back to the sandspit to see if she had overlooked a fork. She hadn't. She paced the limits of the shoal, hunting the entrance to the proper trail. There was only the one.

"Mama! Daddy!" she called. They ought to be able to hear her. The stream wasn't that far from the picnic area. Keep calm.

Silence.

She turned in tight circles, panicky, and screaming furiously for her parents, but they didn't answer. If this was their idea of a joke—! She rushed up the trail again and glared at the log cabin. Only a slabwood door faced the road, and it was shut, but a wisp of smoke rose from the corner chimney.

"Hello!" she demanded. "Is anybody home?"

No one answered. She knocked, civilly at first, then angrily. She took a rock from the roadside and beat against the door with it. There just had to be a person inside, maybe a person asleep, someone to help her find the right trail to camp. Somebody had built a fire in that fireplace, if that was really smoke coming out of the chimney.

In the distance a dog yodeled, a tracking-dog, attacking-dog sound. She felt nervous and cold, and her skin sprouted fresh goosebumps.

There was no outside handle on the slabwood door. When she hunched close, she could see a bar through a crack at the opening edge. The dog bugled again, closer now and keening. She began to whimper. That dog was after her! She was scared of that dog!

"Let me in!" She hammered on the door again. Maybe it was a ranger station where nobody lived, she thought feverishly, where they kept equipment and stuff like that. She had to figure out some way to get in.

She thought to try lifting the bar by poking her finger through, but the crack was too narrow, and her ballpoint pen wouldn't go through either. She searched the ground for a twig slender enough to slide through the space, rigid enough to lift the latchbar.

At last she thought of using the blue plastic clip of her ballpoint pen, and when she tried that, it slid through. She pulled on the doorbrace with one hand to relieve pressure on the latch and nudged the bar with the point of her clip, gently, carefully, so as not to snap the slender plastic. At first it would not move; then the bar gave a little and slowly, slowly eased upward.

Suddenly the door sprang inward. A huge hand reached out and grabbed her by the arm and dragged her inside.

"Eep!" she squealed.

A rough palm covered her mouth; a heavy arm pinned her arms and hauled her back from the door. Somebody else closed the door and secured the latch, and there was darkness. The somebody holding her said "S-s-st!" and then all was still.

-2-

A CABIN WITHOUT WINDOWS

 She fought to get free, she fought for air. It was a mistake. The one holding her clasped her the tighter and further hampered her breathing. She groaned a muffled plea.

"S-s-st!" A threatening shake silenced her. Deep quiet prevailed all around. Despite her terror, she grew conscious of movement inside the room, and presently her vision accommodated to the dim interior. It was a cabin without windows. She could see the corner fireplace and a form that glided between the glowing coals there and her view of them. Then she made out the silhouette of a person stooping slightly and peeping between the logs of the cabin at something, or somebody, outside.

The figure fled noiselessly along the wall to a different observation chink. A hushed voice announced, with a peculiar cadence, "Can't see nobody nowheres." The words sounded almost foreign, and it took her a moment or two to make sense of them.

The massive arms pinioning hers relaxed somewhat. Boy drew a deep, grateful breath into her suffering lungs. The man holding her growled, "You come this place by youself?" with that same foreign cadence; and then

11

harshly, while she was still trying to figure out what he had said, "Won't nobody sides you out there?" Finally she understood him, and she shook her head as best she could.

Reluctantly, it seemed, he unstoppered her mouth but kept a good grip on her arm. She burst into tearful entreaty. "Mister, I need help. I'm trying to find my mama and daddy, and I guess I got on the wrong trail. The trail to the picnic area, could you show me where it is, please Mister?"

For a long time he did not answer her, and she cowered under his sinister, suspicious gaze. He was a gigantic man, taller far than her father, and far more powerfully built. His huge frame seemed designed the way some machines are, for functional strength alone. He had the jaw of an anvil. His skin was very black and pitted; his muddy eyes constantly shifted.

"Where you stay?" he rumbled.

Eagerly she attempted to tell him. "We're at Overlook picnic area, you know, the one just south of where the interstate crosses the parkway. I can show you how to get there from the interstate, if you've got a car."

He appeared to be only half-listening, or perhaps distracted by something else. "Where," he persisted at last, giving her a shake, "*where*?"

"The pipipic—the pic the pic the picnic area," she stuttered in her desire to tell him what he wished to know, "the Bellemont—oh! Where you get off to go there, you mean? Well, if you're driving south on the interstate, you take Exit 9. On the parkway you take the exit marked Bellemont Overlook, and it isn't but a little way—"

Again the puzzled, scarcely attending pause. Didn't he

understand what she was saying? Perhaps her way of talking was as difficult for him as theirs was for her.

The other voice interposed, "Bellemont. Might could be Yancey's boy, Pa."

The speaker was a handsome young lad who approached and peered at her curiously. He was a boy perhaps her own age, muscular and much taller than Boy. He had to stoop to examine her face. Bright eyes looked her up and down. She felt scruffy and ashamed of her bare feet. He fingered the cloth of her stained workshirt. "He been bleeding, Pa," he reported, and he questioned, "You Yancey's boy?"

"Isaac!" the father warned. The lad backed away. "This inster, this inster—stay?"

"Interstate, yes!" Boy responded hopefully. "Exit 9, on the interstate driving south. On the parkway it says Bellemont—"

"You Yancey's boy?" Another fierce shake.

"Why—yes. Yes, Boy's what they call me sometimes, it's just a nickname, though. I'm really a . . ."

"S-s-st!" from Isaac.

In the listening silence that followed came the threatening bay of the hunting dog. Father and son looked at each other across the dim interior of the cabin with no windows. "Tater hole," said the father, with a jerk of his head.

Swiftly Isaac dragged a cornshuck mat from in front of the fireplace and piled to one side some planks that were concealed there, which covered a round, black hole. It resembled nothing so much as a well there in the room.

With his free hand the father snatched up a piece of firewood and stood it like a club in readiness beside the door. Wordlessly, he transferred Boy to the lad, who promptly wrestled her to the brink of the well. At her squawk of protest, he shut her mouth with his hand. He was not heavyset like his father, but he was very strong. They tumbled together into the hole.

They fell awkwardly onto knobby potatoes that smelled of damp earth and rot. Over them, the father replaced the planks and spread them with the cornshuck mat. Once more the cabin lapsed into quiet.

In her ear Isaac whispered, "They hunting for you. Dog'll eat you up."

Hunting for her! Perhaps her parents were—but with a dog? She longed to question him. His warning of danger suggested a willingness to help her.

Outside the cabin the dog yelped and someone banged on the door. "Ike! Big Ike! Open up." "Open up there," ordered a second voice, and yet a different voice added, "We know you in there."

"Who there?" Ike growled.

A gabble of voices answered him and there was the slow rasp of the latchbar being lifted. Some persons, perhaps more than the three who had called, entered the cabin, stamping the dirt floor, shouting at Ike and at one another, moving throughout the tiny enclosure. Several feet tramped over the cornshuck mat of the tater hole, and the quarrelsome, questioning voices and Ike's surly replies rose and fell.

They stamped about the cabin, all talking at the same time again, more jovially now, and soon the conversation converged around the doorway. The dog outside barked several times; one of the men whistled it up and spoke to it, and boasted about it, and gave it some sharp order.

Then the voices diminished in the distance and became at last inaudible.

Long after the voices had ceased, Boy could hear the faint bugling of the dog. When that too subsided, Ike uncovered the tater hole and let them out. At Isaac's eager questioning, he drew the lad aside and swiveled his eyes toward Boy in an odd way. She strained to listen and made out a few mumbled words. "Slave catchers. They run Jeffrey down." He seized the rude club and brooded over it. With one swift, brutal arc he slammed it into the dirt floor. "Run him down," he said again, and this time his voice shook.

-3-

MAKING PLANS

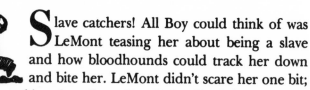

Slave catchers! All Boy could think of was LeMont teasing her about being a slave and how bloodhounds could track her down and bite her. LeMont didn't scare her one bit; he was making that all up. But Ike's talk of slave catchers wasn't teasing, wasn't made up, and his eyes swiveling around at her seemed to implicate her. That was scary. She wanted to ask about the man he called Jeffrey run down by the hunters' dog, but the way he had swung that club made her wary.

Still, something about the hunters' visit altered Ike's mood. He piled logs in the fireplace and fanned up flames that lighted their faces. To Isaac he mumbled an order that brought from the boy a jubilant whoop; he sprang to the door and slipped out. At the hearth, the man busied himself with raking out some smoking black objects that looked like coals but evidently were not. Boy gazed around the cabin's interior.

It was tiny, half the size of her room at home, and except for a bucket and gourd in one corner, unfurnished. Close by the cornshuck mat lay a pile of rags. Other rags hung from pegs on one wall. Dried leaves drooped from open rafters. There was no floor other than the smooth, trampled earth. Yet the miserable shack was made cozy by the stoked fire, and that, and Ike's improved demeanor, heartened her.

"If I could get to the interstate—" she ventured.

Ike slammed a fist into his open palm. "I an't study no insterstess," he roared. He gestured toward the fireplace. "Sit by."

Frightened, she obeyed. She huddled trembling as he stamped about the room with his fists clenched. His great bulk towered over her and she squeezed her eyes shut in dread of what might happen next. But no blow fell. Isaac reentered and knelt before the fire, and Ike moved away.

Isaac held in his hands a scrap of gray fur. "Most nigh chawed thu the trap," he bragged to his father. He proudly showed the girl a limp, dead squirrel. From a crevice in the fireplace, he drew out a broken knife blade. Delicately he honed the worn metal against a flat stone, and as she watched, hacked off the animal's head and gutted and skinned it. He knotted the furry tail at the end of a stick, and tapping a few shimmering coals tidily together, dangled the meager carcass above them.

Entrails sputtered and fried on top of the burning log where he had flung them. The smell of scorching fur assailed her nostrils. Ike paced the room, muttering. She felt queasy and helpless; hopeless, homesick. In all her life, no adult had menaced her the way Ike did. Instead, she had passed her nearly twelve years praised and flattered, listened to, petted, cajoled, coaxed and bribed.

In return, she gave her parents . . . what? Love. Most certainly love; what child could fail to love a mother and father like hers, or to appreciate them? If she sometimes showed indifference to all they did for her, well, that came of the good things always being there; it made a kid take the good things for granted. Her parents understood that; they said so. They didn't expect to be continually thanked just because their kids' lives were so much easier than theirs had been. They realized that kids got bored listening to tales of the old-timey days.

Ike ceased his pacing and squatted beside his son. They debated the state of the roasting squirrel, rotated it on its stick. They pinched the sizzling carcass to test for doneness and licked their blistered fingers, and each jeered at the other's pain and greed. Surging heat caused the limbs of the carcass to curl outwards. After much testing and consulting, they at last pronounced the meat done, and Isaac laid out the charred morsel on the hearthstone. With exquisite care, he sectioned it into three equal parts.

Ike took a portion up and began devouring it. Isaac, with a glance at Boy, indicated the two remaining. She stared into the flames and pretended not to see. He speared one of the chunks with the knife blade and proffered it. "Eat. Good." He rubbed his lean belly as he spoke, as one might to a backward child. When she shook her head, he took his portion and began eating ravenously, holding it with both hands and licking the grease that ran between his fingers.

The meat showed red; it just couldn't be cooked through. Isaac and his father gnawed the gristle loose from the joints and sucked the bones clean. They exactly divided between them the portion she had declined and ate that, and when the last shred disappeared, Isaac sighed and reached for the round black objects on the hearth. He broke one open and held it out to Boy. It was a potato, baked among the ashes, but even so bland an offering made her stomach lurch. In her fearful uncertainty, she felt as though she could never eat again, ever.

Ike stood up and broke off a few dried leaves from one of the bunches hanging in the rafters. They crumbled herb flakes onto the baked potatoes before wolfing them down, dusty jackets and all. They talked with their mouths full, discussing something that concerned her, she felt sure, for they kept glancing at her as they carried on their furtive debate. Isaac rose and strolled to the bucket in the corner. He dipped the gourd and brought it filled with water for Boy to drink.

Water. Her dry mouth creaked with thirst. Isaac's dirty, greasy thumb hooked right into the water, and an oily slick swirled about some bits of straw floating on the surface. She said in disgust, "Nice. Real sanitary. You sure you don't want to spit in it too?"

If she offended him, he gave no sign. Perhaps he had not understood. He nodded encouragement and said with simple courtesy, "Might be you like some water."

His kindly words so shamed her that she took the dipper in her hands. When she turned back to Ike she drank greedily, the whole gourdful. Afterward she sat for a long while clasping the smooth shell. The hot fire stung her cheeks; she was uncomfortable, but she would not move back, lest they see the tears that streamed down her cheeks. Her throat ached from her silent weeping for Mama and Daddy.

Ike and Isaac muttered on and on. They seemed to be making plans of some sort. She thought of her parents out in these mountains, frantic with worry about her, and the realization that these people did not care—indeed, they prevented her from returning to them—so angered her that her spirits revived. Tears ceased welling in her eyes. She wiped her nose on her shirtsleeve and began making plans of her own. For a long time she stared into the empty gourd, plotting, while the man and boy grumbled on, unnoticing. Once outside that door, if she got a head start on them . . .

She stood up, feigning bashfulness. "I got to pee," she simpered.

Ike gave a snort. "Go pee."

Simple as that! Her ruse had worked. Once outside that door, she would race for the laurel clumps and hide among them until they came out to look for her. They would expect her to flee along the road that ran past the cabin. When they gave up pursuit and went back in the house, she could safely follow the track until she found some help. That road was bound to lead her somewhere.

She replaced the gourd in its bucket, moved with false nonchalance to the door, lifted the latchbar and stepped outside.

It was dark. Black night dark! No wonder Ike hadn't tried to stop her. But what had become of the day? She felt disoriented and she closed and opened her eyes several times to make sure she had not gone blind. No stars shone. The dark came earlier in the mountains, she told herself, but not as early as this.

The air lay heavy and cold upon her. Her feet were freezing as she picked her way around the cabin. In one or two places where mud chinking had fallen away, firelight shone through. She peeped through a crack and saw Ike plucking a large leaf from one of the bunches in the rafters. She moved on.

Behind the cabin, downslope, a tiny hut loomed, undoubtedly the privy. But other objects she could not identify also loomed, possibly only underbrush, but forbidding enough to prevent her approaching the outhouse. She stepped a little apart from the cabin, unbuttoned her jeans and relieved herself.

She would have to wait until morning for her escape. She didn't have it in her to investigate that privy, and she certainly lacked the nerve to explore the mountain on a cold, dark night.

When she reentered the cabin, Ike was sitting cross-legged before the fire, folding his leaf into a tight packet. Isaac knelt a little to one side and scratched stick figures in the dirt with her blue plastic pocket clip. He returned the clip to her, smiling shyly, and she, as a token of truce, used it to label his smallest figure *BOY.*

Isaac studied the markings. "What that be?"

"You ought to know. You're the one that drew the picture. I figured you meant it was a girl called Boy."

He stared at her blankly. "Gurkoboy?"

He still didn't realize she was a girl, the nerd. "It's my i-ni-tials," she pronounced.

He bent close to the letters. "What be's nish—nish—?"

"Initials, Dr. Einstein. Initials that stand for my name." These people were dumb, she told herself, really, really dumb. She had heard there were illiterates in these mountains, still living the way people did in the Dark Ages. For all she knew, these two still believed in slavery. She oughtn't to have much trouble getting away from such retards tomorrow. She explained contemptuously, "My initials spell Boy. Get it? They call me Boy."

He shrugged. "Call me boy too. Name Isaac. How you name?"

What a lamebrain! "Boy's my name," she said arrogantly. "That's what they call me, and that's what my name is."

"Boy," said Ike, "git over here." He spat a rich, brown stream of juice into the fireplace.

Shrinking, she went up to him, all arrogance dispelled. He took her wrist in his great paw and looked it over, pushing up her sleeve for a better examination. Astounded, she too looked at ugly cuts and scratches patterning her flesh. Ike chewed solemnly, drooled a bubbly supply of brown juice onto the back of her hand, and from this reservoir, applied it to the wounds on her arms and legs, to her gouged cheek. "Baccy draw the pizen," he commented.

When Ike had finished doctoring her wounds, he let her go and began banking the fire. Isaac stepped as if by signal to the pile of rags and divided them the way he had sectioned the squirrel, into three equal portions. To Boy he assigned a dingy blanket made of faded, worn garments stitched together and quilted in layers. A long, gray-striped shirt at one corner must have been one of Isaac's, outgrown.

The man dropped to his knees and indicated that the two younger ones should do the same. They knelt three in a line before the fireplace, and the man began praying in the mumbled dialect that Boy found so hard to understand. She was not accustomed to prayers being said aloud, except in church and at her Mamaw Overtha's table. She managed to decipher a few words.

"Freedom," Ike prayed sonorously, and "Lead us,

Father," and she thought of her own father and ached with longing for her mother, and tears began slipping once more down her cheeks.

Afterwards, bundled snuffling inside the lumpy quilt, she forced herself to calm down, and for the first time seriously pondered her predicament. *Why was she here?* By the light of the dwindling fire, she could see Isaac's face collapsed in slumber. Across the room Ike snorted and snored. Who were these strangers, and why were they holding her? They had not searched her, had not demanded money from her. She didn't have any money.

But Mama and Daddy did!

It wasn't like they were millionaires, really rich people; still they had money enough to buy just about anything they wanted. Anyone who paid the slightest attention could tell they would spend every cent they had on their children if that were necessary.

Now, just suppose Ike and his son were bandits hiding out in these mountains and were holding her for ransom.

She knew right away she had found the answer. It explained why Ike shoved her into the tater hole and why those men and their dog were out hunting for her. Mama and Daddy must be frantic with worry about her!

It was a relief just to understand what had happened to her. She immediately felt much better for having figured the mess out. That was the way it always was with her—maybe with everybody—and she began plotting how she was going to escape as soon as morning came and she could see where to run. That road in front of the cabin. It had to lead somewhere, probably to the interstate, and sooner or later she would meet a car that she could flag down and ask for help.

Actually, she alone was to blame for taking the wrong trail to the picnic area this morning, but that was a mistake anybody might have made; and she had been so mad at LeMont for swiping her sneakers she forgot to watch where she was going.

She decided it was stupid to reproach herself for an ordinary mistake, even though it still struck her as odd. There were some other odd things she couldn't account for either, like the night coming on too quickly and that posse out hunting for her—but these were details she was foolish to try and figure out right now, when she needed to concentrate on her escape.

Tomorrow, she schemed, as soon as morning came, she would pretend she was going out to the privy ... or should she wait until Ike went to the privy? Or perhaps she could confide in Isaac? He acted friendly, and she might find out that none of this was as complicated as it seemed, tomorrow morning. Tomorrow. Her thoughts went round and round, scheming for tomorrow. At last, exhausted, she slept.

– 4 –

ESCAPE

"Snow!" said Isaac when he opened the door the next morning. "Oh, Pa, it snowed in the night. What we going to do now?"

The man looked out. "It's quit," he said, "but maybe it start up again." For a long time he stood in the open doorway and studied the sullen sky. Isaac, beside him, watched his face.

Boy lay tense in her nest, wakened by their voices. They assumed she was still asleep, and she wished she were, because there for a while their voices had been transformed into the persuasive, caressing tones of Mama and Daddy, saying the crazy, illogical things you accepted as reasonable in a dream. Daddy was going to scramble some eggs with a helicopter, and Mama said rapidly, in her questioning way, "Hot chocolate? Pancakes? Waffles? Muffins?" and Daddy said oatmeal stuck to your ribs at a picnic snow, at a picnic snow; and very soon after that Boy looked up and realized what the new day's first calamity was. Still, snow might help her, she decided, if enough of it fell to cover her tracks.

"Going to snow some more." Big Ike spoke her

thoughts. "You get ready." He stepped outside and closed the door behind him.

Isaac leaped into action. He rolled aside last night's un-eaten potatoes. He piled logs in the fireplace. He jumped into the tater hole and threw yams alongside last night's banked coals; and while he worked, Boy sat up and thought about that snow-covered road outside. She hugged her blanket around her and strolled toward the door, faking a yawn.

Isaac looked at her and said warningly, "Snow out there. Pa gone up the big house."

"I don't care where he's gone. I've got to use the facility."

"You better fix you feet." He took down some rags from one of the pegs and showed her how to wrap her feet. "Twon't get you far," he suggested.

"So?" she said. "It'll get me to the crapper, won't it?"

Outside the cabin, Big Ike's footsteps trailed up the road. She tramped after him, setting each bandaged foot carefully in his tracks. Where the road turned, she hesitated. She lifted aside some laden branches and crept into a rhododendron hedge.

Ike had gone to the big house, wherever that was, and whether for a few minutes, an hour or the day, she had no way of knowing. But with the blanket to keep her warm, she could wait him out. She pushed farther in, moving as few branches as possible and stopping often to listen. Snow had stilled the forest. In this pale, upholstered world the only sound that came to her was her own breathing. Drifts weighed down branches and vines and opened a path for her.

Before long she glimpsed a clearing beyond the

branches of rhododendron, and in this open area, not fifty paces from where she crouched, a farmhouse.

Big Ike stood in front of the farmhouse, his giant shoulders rounded in an attitude of subservience. A white woman, wearing a long skirt and shawl, crossed a narrow porch and handed something to him; he ducked his head in response and evidently spoke, for his breath condensed in a puff of white above his head. The woman went back into her house. Ike waited humbly.

It was a nondescript Carolina farmhouse, like others Boy had seen all her life in the countryside around Freetown and back in the mountains, a shambling, weatherboarded dwelling of perhaps three or four rooms, set on creek-rock piers, with a single paned window on each side and a rusting metal roof that extended over the lean-to porch. This, she couldn't help thinking, *this* was the big house?

The woman returned to the porch with her arms full. She piled her load into Ike's outstretched arms. He ducked his head and backed away. She watched after him for a minute with her arms akimbo; then she went into the house and closed the door.

A woman! Another human being was alive in these woods, somebody Boy could ask for help! She clutched the quilt around her and got set to make her dash. She wanted to be sure there was no chance of Ike rushing back and grabbing her before she got in her appeal to the farmer woman. When she reckoned he must have retreated far enough, she assessed the snow-laden bushes in front of her for the best way of getting around or through them. Around, she told herself; *now*; she plunged forward.

And fell. Something pinned her face down. Ike's voice

grated in her ear, "Don't make no racket or you cotch it. Git up."

She had missed her chance. Through her own stupid miscalculation, she had waited too long. She struggled to her feet, spitting out snow and scraping the burning cold from her cheeks. Big Ike prodded her back to the road. The bundles the woman had given him lay where he had dumped them. There were two cloth sacks tied at their necks with string, and there were two pairs of work boots fastened together by their laces. A bundle of clothing buttoned into a shirt had broken apart.

"You carry these," said Ike. He thrust the cloth sacks into her hands. Swiftly he gathered up the shoes and spilled clothing. "Git." She plodded back to the cabin.

Isaac had been watching for their return. He flung wide the cabin door and yelled, "Christmas gift!"

"Christmas gift," his father echoed in his harsh voice.

Boy set down the bags and glared at the father, then at the son. Did they expect her to swallow that, Christmas in the middle of August? She had to admit it didn't feel like August outdoors; it felt like winter, and the snow heaped on the mountainside certainly created a Christmas-card scene.

Maybe the cold had drugged her and made her feel like this, queer and displaced, like a person with amnesia who forgets everything for months and can't figure out why it's suddenly Christmas ... Christmas, and cold, and the weird dark last night, when it should have been noon—Details! she scolded herself in agitation. She simply must not think about details at a time like this. She had to concentrate on what was happening right now, so she could escape. She could figure out the details later.

By the light of leaping flames, Isaac was examining the bundle of clothing the farmer woman had loaded into Ike's arms. There was a new shirt for him in the lot and one for his father. They had each received new trousers and boots, and there was in addition an old-fashioned wool frock coat that showed considerable wear.

Isaac immediately tried the new clothes on over his worn garments and stamped around in the stiff, brass-toed boots. He tried on the frock coat too. His wrists extended well beyond its frayed cuffs and there were two buttons missing, but the coat's finer fabric and cut made the other new clothing look coarse and poor by comparison. Isaac strutted and capered in his finery. Big Ike actually smiled at his posturing, and there for a moment in the cheerful light of the fireplace, a trace of fatherly pride blurred the hard lines of his face.

The moment passed. Ike turned to the fireplace and poked at the roasting yams with the knife blade, which seemed to be their sole cooking implement. He picked up two of last night's potatoes and gave Boy and Isaac each one. "Eat your breakfast," he ordered. "We got a long way to go."

Oatmeal? Hot chocolate? Boy thought fleetingly, as in her dream; but following her long fast, even the grayed flesh of the cold potato looked good, and she took a bite. It tasted marvelous. She devoured it, took another and eyed the portions jealously when Ike divided the last potato among them. After they had eaten, Ike drew from inside his shirt a fold of oiled paper.

"Candy!" Isaac danced ecstatically around the room.

Ike dispensed sticky chunks from the paper, one for each.

A Girl Called Boy

Isaac begged with his mouth full of taffy, "Nother one! Spare us nother one, do, Pa. For Christmas, please!"

But Ike was adamant. He refolded the packet and stowed it inside his shirt. "You got candy in you mouth," he admonished. "Eat it all now and you got nothing to look forward to."

The rich syrup spreading in her mouth improved Boy's spirits, and food in her stomach restored her confidence. She said to Isaac, "Today isn't Christmas—" but when he stared her down, she qualified, "—is it?"

"Course it Christmas! Yu spect us get new clothes and wheat flour and candy any day sides Christmas?"

His self-assurance shook her. She dropped her head and moved away from him so he couldn't see the terror in her eyes. She wanted to cry; she was determined not to cry. She struggled to make herself listen to him mumbling something to his father, but it was no use. She couldn't go on pretending; she had to face the truth: it really was Christmas. Somehow she had lost track of time. Something strange and awful had happened to her, and she didn't know what it was.

Unexpectedly Isaac touched her arm, and she whirled around, trembling. She was aware of Ike peering curiously at her from over his shoulder.

"For you," said Isaac's mild voice.

She said wildly, "What? What do you mean? I don't know what you're talking about!" Then she saw that he held out to her a small packet of folded oiled paper.

"Candy," he said, in that same soft voice. "From us'ns, cause you didn't get no Christmas."

"I don't want any of your Christmas!" But of course he couldn't know how close to panic she was. She tried to patch that up. "You keep it for yourself. I already had all I want."

Still he offered the packet, and at last, because she could not bear the pity in his eyes, she took it from him and tore at the paper. There were two small pieces of taffy inside. She took one and stuck it in her mouth. "We'll share," she said, on a strangled note, and shoved the other sweet back into his hand.

Before Isaac could answer, she strode to the bucket in the corner and washed the taffy down with a swallow of water. For a long time afterward she imagined she felt it moving sluggishly through her gullet and coming at last to rest, a sticky, heavy mass in her stomach.

Big Ike busied himself rolling his new clothes into a bundle together with his bed rags. The knife blade he placed in his shirt, in some sort of pocket sewed there. "Time to get gone," he told his son, and Isaac began assembling his belongings. To Boy he presented his discarded shoes. "You can't get nowhere in the snow thout shoes," he remarked.

They were ankle boots, metal-capped and laced with thongs. One had cracked across the toe and lacked its tongue, but she gladly accepted his gift. She sat on the floor and pulled them over the makeshift wrappings Isaac had helped her with earlier. The cumbersome bandages made them fit not too badly, although she flapped when she walked, like a clown.

"You can have this, too." He stripped off the frock coat.

"Oh, I couldn't! Not your new coat!" She objected sincerely, remembering how proudly he had modeled it, and she added a harmless fib. "It looks so nice on you."

"I got another one." Sure enough he did. A rag taken

from one of the pegs proved to be a jacket, worn through at the elbows, to be sure, but it was made of wool and had a complete set of wooden buttons.

Boy put on the coat. Its sleeves hid her hands, and the skirt fell almost to her ankles, but like the shoes Isaac had given her, it meant protection against the cold. She wasn't going to abandon the idea of escape, but right now it was more important to think of survival. "Where are we going?" she inquired timidly.

"To Freetown," she understood Isaac to answer; but before she could ask him to repeat the name, Big Ike interposed, "to freedom, that's where we going to. Running to freedom."

–5–

LONG SHADOWS OF WINTER

By the time they set out, it was snowing hard. Ike nodded satisfaction and said the blizzard would cover their tracks. They skulked past the privy and down the mountain for a short distance; then abruptly he led them in among trees to where a stream ran black between snowy banks. Here Ike bade them take their shoes off and wade.

"But it's freezing!" Boy protested.

"You get used to it," Ike told her.

"I don't want to get used to it. Why, I could die of the cold."

He said ominously, "You might die something else."

Isaac had already rolled his trouser legs and stoically splashed downstream, his shoes dangling from the laces knotted and slung around his neck.

Boy took one despairing look at Ike's closed face and removed her shoes. The icy stab of her first step stopped her on one leg in the stream, transfixed, an incongruous winter heron.

"Git," said Ike.

She took the second step. Cold cramps knotted her muscles. She decided she could not bear to go on, but a sharp blow between her shoulder blades persuaded her. She hobbled forward, Big Ike huffing and mumbling close behind. A dull ache rose in her limbs and she could think of nothing but her suffering. She groaned piteously and Ike snarled. Her legs at the waterline burned like fire, like fire; she yearned for fire to leap into; she fantasized that a terrible burn from a fire could feel no worse than the burn of that icy water; her calves lost feeling. Presently she realized she was not all that uncomfortable. Big Ike was right—she had gotten used to it.

Far downstream, Ike permitted them to leave the water and put their shoes back on. He led them into a section of cut-over woods, and they trudged in silence for what seemed like hours.

It had stopped snowing. Boy's feet ached almost as much in warming up as they had in going numb. But her heart pumped stoutly, her body slowly adjusted to the cold and at last she no longer felt chilled.

She had been assigned, together with her bedroll, to carry the roasted yams for their journey, pulled from the coals at the last moment and rolled into a gunnysack. Copying the others, she slung her burden across a shoulder to make the traveling easier. Gradually she shifted the load so that the bedroll rested on her back and she could hug the warm potatoes to her chest. She dropped back to speak to Isaac, bringing up the rear.

"Why did he make us wade downstream that way?"

"So's to thow the dog off, if they set it on us."

Something suffocating rose ponderously in her chest and threatened her breathing. "Who would set a dog on us?"

He laughed without humor. "Slave catcher."

"Are you kidding me?"

Ahead, Big Ike raised an angry fist. "Don't talk!"

They hurried on.

She stumbled along drunkenly, her feet and legs all at once uncoordinated by the churning of her thoughts. It was just as well that Ike had forbidden conversation, because it would take a while for her to sort out her confused perceptions. She could conceivably have been mistaken about what she had overheard back at the cabin, about the slave catchers running down Jeffrey, but there was no mistaking what Isaac had just told her. *Slave catcher!* They were fleeing the slave catcher. These fellows actually believed they were slaves, and obviously they assumed she was a slave too. After all, she was black, and didn't she tell them herself she was Yancey's boy?

But she was Boy Yancey, not Yancey's boy! It was all a dreadful mistake, a mistake that fitted in with the silly notion that had come to her when she stood on Bellemont Overlook. Then, having thought of that again, the notion spun round and round in her head, a roulette ball that would not come to rest. Suppose freedom *was* a trick? Suppose in that brick mansion overlooking the lake Yanceys lived yet, attended by their slaves? Suppose she—just suppose—

She reeled forward, sweaty and breathless.

The sun broke through. Snow mantling the mountain dwindled and became patchy as they proceeded downward. On the other side of a ridge there was no snow at all. Here they moved along rapidly for miles on a washed-out logging road. Boy grew tired. She tried to guess the time by the sun. It hung so low in the sky it appeared to be setting rather than approaching its zenith.

"Dinnertime," Ike announced.

She halted thankfully. Food, warmth, rest—

"You got our dinner," Ike reminded her over his shoulder.

She faltered, "Aren't we going to sit down?" But plainly he meant them to keep walking while they ate.

She fumbled with the gunnysack and passed yams to her companions. Her portion was barely warm now, and it was half-cooked; and she was so tired that the very act of chewing seemed unendurable. She dragged along in her paddle-foot shoes, and Ike said harshly, "Move along there!" She felt tears slide down her face. Mistake. Her cheeks stung and burned from the salt. She clamped her teeth around the last mouthful, shouldered the gunnysack again and wiped her eyes and nose and wet cheeks on her sleeve. The stiff wool chafed her skin.

Isaac swung along beside her. "Don't cry," he said. "You daddy be all right."

She faced him, startled. "Why do you say that? What do you know about my daddy?"

Thud. She plowed into Ike, halted in the road.

"No talk, I say." Though he whispered, his expression lent thunder and lightning to his words. "And this be the last time I say."

He was so mean. He acted like he hated her. If he hated her that bad, why did he make her come with them?

For money. Of course!

The bewildering events of the morning had made her forget about him being a kidnapper, holding her for ransom. Now she went back to that shrewd guess of hers and found it a welcome, almost comforting thought, like finding one familiar face in a crowd. And it fit. *Slave catcher* was just their code word for all the people out hunting her, her parents, the police, the hunters and their dog. There was no such thing as slavery anymore. This was North Carolina; this was America!

She forgot her fatigue and marched onward, alert and scheming. They were dimwits, her captors. All she needed was one good opportunity.

In the afternoon, when they forded a creek, she saw bright blood oozing from raw places on Isaac's heels. "New shoes," he said with a rueful smile. Uncomplaining, he tore strips from his bedding and wrapped his feet.

On and on they followed the road that hairpinned down to the valley. They walked in tall, sighing forests of pine and in stark and silent forests of leafless hardwoods. Twice more they forded mountain streams, and once they crossed on stepping stones below a delicate waterfall, threading out of a rocky glen, that rose in folds above their heads higher and higher and higher until its beginning was muffled in mountain greenery.

Boy looked around for some container to drink from, but there were no discarded beer cans here, no bottles or poptop rings, no decaying McDonald's cups, no Kentucky Fried tubs—no sign at all of human visitation. The absence of trash made her feel uneasy. How in the world had hikers missed finding this beautiful waterfall? Too isolated, perhaps. Yet not much farther along the road they came across a field of broken brown cornstalks, evidence of civilization. They scuttled past.

After the cornfield, the road improved. Some washed-out places had been filled in with stones, and there was the bright new wood of recent repairs on a narrow bridge they crossed. But they didn't meet any cars, and Boy wondered about that. On the crummiest backroads in the mountains, you usually met a pickup or two, with a hunter driving and gunracks across his rear window, and maybe a bluetick hound standing and riding the bumps in the bed of the pickup.

Hunters and gunracks made Boy nervous. Even if they met a pickup, she wasn't sure she would have the courage to flag it down for help. Better wait for the pickup to come along before deciding, she told herself. As it turned out, they didn't stay on the improved part of the road long enough to require a decision.

When the topmost pine of the western mountains nicked the sun, they came upon another field, this one plowed and fenced with rails. Here they left the logging road and moved along a stream that ran full-banked in the forest. The walking was easy. Underbrush had been cleared, and the ground gave gently underfoot.

Something white glimmered ahead of them; a flash of light made Boy blink. The forest opened out and she saw the reason for the flash—final rays of the sun striking against a windowpane. Ike bent over and slithered through the trees, motioning them to hurry. "Till us get past the big house," he muttered.

Boy got a good look at it. This was more like a big house—a white-painted, two-story dwelling with box-woods nestling around the high porch. It was not pretentious, but it was large enough to be suitably called a big house, and she began at once plotting a way of getting to it. There would be civilized people inside a house like that, peope who would rescue her.

Ike clutched her wrist and yanked her along.

Past the big house, well hidden behind a buffer planting

of hollies and barberry, there were stables and a small cowshed enclosed by a split-rail fence. Here also a row of log huts huddled together, huts windowless like tobacco barns, but smaller and lower, and each with its own mud chimney. Two of the chimneys sent forth smoky signals of occupancy.

Ike entered the largest cabin without knocking. A stout black woman stood with him in the doorway and pointed out another cabin from which smoke rose. The door of the latter did not yield to his touch and he rapped urgently. Someone inside lifted the bar; someone exclaimed upon seeing him and flung the door wide. As they crossed the threshold, a grizzled little old man with a comical smile welcomed them into a crowded room.

-6-

CHRISTMAS FROLIC

I t was a mean little cabin they entered, built of crooked logs and lighted only by the fireplace. Except for a bed frame pegged to the wall and a rude plank table, the room contained no furniture.

But laughter and music enriched the poor dwelling. A tiny orchestra performed in the corner opposite the fireplace. One musician plinked on a banjo made from a large gourd. A man almost as big as Ike played harmonica, and there were besides quill pipes and cymbals improvised from pot covers. A crosseyed boy clicked a pair of bleached white rib bones together. He made a lewd gesture at Boy as they entered. She turned her back.

The men in the cabin crowded around Ike, shaking him by the hand, shaking him by the arm, and the little old man with the comical smile grabbed both his arms and worried him affectionately.

Ike smiled in an almost human way. "Uncle Jim. Aunt Jenny."

The ancient woman he addressed gathered him and Isaac into her arms and whispered to them. Tears glittered in her eyes.

"Oh, Muh—my Muh," Isaac quavered.

Ike stood rigid. A small muscle dimpled his jaw. His eyes stared dully at nothing. After a space, however, he blinked and turned away from Aunt Jenny and surveyed the crowd, counting.

"It's mostly our people in here," said old Uncle Jim. He patted the air soothingly. "There's some come down from Cedar Springs to look after their white folks over Christmas, but them'uns at the big house won't pick you out in this lot. Do they look in, they think you the Cedar Springs help. Cedar folks figure you belong the big house."

"Sit down, son, sit down, eat you some supper." It was Aunt Jenny at Boy's elbow. She offered a wooden trencher filled with mashed October beans and collards. "I got pone baking, too, and they's molasses." By the time Boy spooned up the last of the beans, Aunt Jenny had brought the hot pone in her apron. "Now, you sop up the pot likker with thishere, and they's molasses in at-ere bucket make you call it the best Christmas rations ever you et." She watched the famished girl sucking her fingers. "Hear tell you Yancey's boy."

"Oh! Yes, ma'am!" She knew it was foolish, how she still had hope. "Oh, ma'am, do you know my mama and daddy? Can you help me . . . ?"

"Shh-sshh. No, son, I don't know 'em, I know *bout* 'em. They be finely." Aunt Jenny's eyes evaded hers. "Best not go talking bout 'em, start youself fretting and everbody else too." She laid an arm across Boy's shoulders. "Eat you some molasses, son, you feel better after you eat good. Everything's worrisome on a holler belly."

She moved away to carry pone to Ike and his son. Boy

watched her gentle Isaac in the same comforting fashion.

She did feel better, a lot better, after eating. Food nourished her curiosity in the room's activity. None of her lifetime had she spent with poor people, really poor people like these. Dirt floor, makeshift furnishings, no electricity—was this the poverty her parents bragged about having known in their youth? But this poverty wasn't boring! The people were all doing interesting things—cooking, making music, joking, whittling. Two little boys played a game like checkers on a square marked out on the dirt floor. Two little girls compared dolls. Boy approached the latter. "Did old Santa bring you your dolls?"

The little girls stared. They clutched dolls made from cornshucks tied with string to form arms, legs, featureless heads. One doll was attired in a scrap of red cloth wrapped around like a shawl; the other wore a bit of figured brown. "Where did you get your dolls?" she asked.

One tot backed away, but the other spoke out bravely. "We didn't steal them—our Mam made them. We didn't steal them."

At home there was a chestful of discarded dolls from years past, Barbie; Ken; baby dolls; character dolls; talking, walking, weeping, wetting dolls. You can have all those dolls, Boy longed to tell these poor mites. Let me give you my dolls.

Rosalie, mother of the children, stepped forward and folded them in her long skirt. She said in a kindly way, "Best you not fool with the girls, son. Go play with the boys, why don't you?"

The crosseyed boy snickered in her face. "Hee-hee-hee!"

Boy's face went hot. She turned her back on the cross-eyed boy. Among these simple folk, of course it would be unseemly for a boy to play dolls with little girls. How she regretted that hasty pretense that made her a boy! I'm a *girl*, she wanted to tell someone, anyone; but everyone in this room was either busy or talking to somebody else. She would feel like a fool walking up to Aunt Jenny, now engaged in pounding some blackened kernels between two stones, and blurting out, "Hey, guess what, I'm really a girl."

Feeling left out, she made another attempt. To the boys, intense over their checkerboard, she said, ever so casually, "Who's winning?"

They gawked at her with solemn, round eyes and did not answer. After a moment she moved away, but she saw one nudge the other, giggling, while with a gesture denoting the halfwit he wound an imbecilic finger at his temple. Maybe he was right. Maybe she really had gone nuts. She felt so lonesome, so lost.

Uncle Jim commanded, "S-ssh!" The room hushed briefly; then at his signal the musicians played louder and livelier, and the little boys leaped to their feet and began jigging. Ike appeared at Boy's side. "Dance!" he growled in her ear. She wanted to ask why, but he gave her a dangerous poke. "Dance," and she shuffled clumsily in her clownish shoes.

The cabin door squawked open in its wooden hinges. A white man accompanied by a little girl in a long, ruffled dress stepped inside. The child carried an important-looking cake, iced with pink frosting and nicely stuck over with candied cherries.

"Well, Uncle Jim," said the man jovially.

"Yessah!" Uncle Jim ducked his head. "Yes*sah*!" He raised a hand to the crowd. The music subsided and the people huddled, respectfully facing the visitors.

"No no no, don't stop. That's what we came for. Little Missy here brought you a prize for your cakewalk. Go on with your frolic."

The little girl set the cake on the floor. Her father smiled paternally, and pulling a rolled newspaper from his back pocket, slapped out a lively rhythm. The musicians picked up the beat of his newspaper, and the little boys began strutting around the cake. Bystanders started clapping. Boy, endeavouring to melt into the crowd, jostled the crosseyed boy. With a curse he returned a vicious shove that propelled her into the ring of dancers; she staggered, but once more began her ungainly shuffle.

Dancing gave her the opportunity to examine the visitors without appearing to, she soon discovered, so she quickened her pace and slapped her feet and whirled and popped her fingers with more purpose.

They were dressed in party clothes, the man in a pleated white shirt that made Boy think of her father in his dinner jacket. The little girl's ruffled calico dress looked very much like one of Boy's own. She was a pretty and gentle-eyed child, about eight or nine years old, obviously captivated by the cakewalk. Joyfully, she patted her hands together.

The girl's father engaged Uncle Jim in conversation. Uncle Jim's servile bowing made them look like caricatures of master and slave from long ago. The master image appealed to Boy: here were civilized people who could help her. She danced and flapped her shoes grotesquely, courting the little girl. The child laughed aloud. "That skinny one," she tugged her father's sleeve and pointed at Boy, "he takes the cake."

"Don't be hasty," said her father. "Give some of the others a chance at it."

Boy danced in a deliberate ring. She plotted. Closer and closer she circled. The child looked meltingly into her eyes and smiled.

"Help me," said Boy, grabbing her hand, "I've been kidnapped—"

The child screamed. "Take your filthy hands off of me, you boy!"

"Who you calling boy?" Boy flared back.

The man thrust his daughter behind him. "What you mean, boy?" he thundered and raised his fist.

Instead, Ike carried out his threat. With one blow he flattened Boy and shoved her with his boot as she fell. "Learn you to lay hands on white folks." She scrabbled on all fours into the crowd.

"He tetch, sah," Ike explained obsequiously, "tetch in he head—" and with his finger he described an imbecilic circle at his own temple.

"Who you?" the man demanded. "Who that boy? Y'all from Cedar Springs?"

"Yes, sah," Uncle Jim interposed, "come see his folks for Christmas—"

"Plague his folks! Get him out of here!"

"Sah."

The man crooned to his daughter. "Don't you make no never mind, Sugar. That just a old crazy boy don't belong here. You, Uncle Jim, cart that halfwit back to Cedar in the morning, hear?"

"Sah."

"Mind, I want that loony on the wagon, first thing in the morning, hear?"

"*Sah.*"

As soon as the door closed behind the man and child, the musicians dropped their instruments, and everybody rushed to crowd around Aunt Jenny, who bore the prize cake to the table. Boy, shunned by all, sulked at one end of the fireplace. She wasn't crazy; they were the crazy ones, a stupid lot of Uncle Toms, letting a white man order them around like that. It was a wonder slavery ever ended in America. Rage assailed her, but rage competed with fear, and with pain too, for Ike's fist and his heavy boot had left real bruises. She flexed her knee, testing the hurt leg, tried a cautious step—and trod on the shock of her life.

The master's newspaper, dropped in the disturbance, had evidently been swept along in Boy's scrambling retreat. Now, at her foot, the name *OVERTHA*—her name—leaped to her eye from the printed page. She snatched up the paper and read in the flickering light,

---

$25 REWARD, from the subscriber. Ranaway or stolen, my Negro girl OVERTHA. She is about 12 years old, small for her age, being but 4 foot 3 or 4 inches high. She is quite plausible when spoken to, but can be recognized by a fresh Y brand on her cheek (which cheek not recollected). Her mother belongs to Mr. Isenhour in Freetown, and she may be lurking in that neighborhood. The above reward will be paid for proof to convict any white person of taking her away or harboring her; or $10 for her apprehension and delivery in some safe jail, where I can get her.

James Yancey

Boy felt suddenly dizzy. She fingered the crusting wound on her cheek. But I'm kidnapped, she agonized. I'm not a slave; nobody's a slave in America. I've been kidnapped!

The symbol of a tiny, fleeing black figure was printed above her name in the classified ads. Old-fashioned objects marked other ads—a carriage, a high-buttoned boot, a top hat. Boy's dazzled eyes picked out a second running figure, and a third and fourth: $100 Reward for my fellow Jeffrey; $50 Reward for LeMont; RANAWAY! RANA-WAY!! RANAWAY!!! Print dimmed and brightened on the page, words blurred and burst and she wondered if she were going crazy.

"You gone crazy?" a hoarse voice cawed in her ear.

Despairingly, she half-nodded.

"How come you steal the master's paper? Get you in trouble and us'ns too." It was Isaac, accusing her.

"I didn't steal it; he dropped it. Oh, Isaac, my name, it's in this newspaper, it says I ran away...."

Isaac pushed her into the corner. "You read it?" he whispered. "You can read?" He snapped his fingers softly. "I hear tell that! They say Mistis Yancey spoil all her slaves, say she got a pet boy she teached writing to! Gimme that. I'll slip it to Uncle Jim, get him run it up to Master fore he miss it and blame the wrong people."

"I've got to read it again first." Boy studied the newspaper one more time. The advertisement described her exactly. It was a sleazy newspaper, a single, cheap, folded sheet, with smeared type. She opened it out enough to read the dateline at the top: Friday, December 23, 1853.

"Gimme," said Isaac urgently. He seized the paper and went to look for Uncle Jim.

Boy sat down slowly at the end of the fireplace. She felt

surprisingly calm. Mama always said that when you're at the bottom, the only way is up. Well, from now on she would be heading up, because this sure was bottom. But in a way it was exciting, too, for now she knew. Somehow she had become trapped in the nineteenth century, in the year 1853!

-7-

READING AND WRITING

Aunt Jenny had placed the pink cake on the plank table, and now she proceeded to divide it among the merrymakers. The smallest children nosed the table and were promised the taste of Uncle Jim's leather strap rather than cake if they touched a single errant crumb. So carefully was the cake divided, so frugally shorn, that few crumbs fell within their temptation. The first and largest slices went to the men, and after them, the women. Children were served last.

Gump, the crosseyed boy, licked crumbs out of one hand while with the other he dangled Boy's slice before her eyes. "You don't get none," he taunted.

"How come?" Isaac demanded. "Aunt Jenny said it was for Boy."

"Learn him not to go layen hands on white folks, that's how come. But I spect Miz Yancey give him so many good cakes, thisn taste like middlings." He waved the pink wedge under Boy's nose. "Mebbe *little* bettern middlings," and licking around a cherry, "Oh-h-h, I wish you taste this good cake."

Deftly Isaac swept the slice out of his hand.

"Hey! You give me back my cake!" Gump yelled.

"Whose cake, Gump?" said Isaac innocently. "I don't see no cake of yours."

"That's my cake—you stole my cake!"

"No, I never stole your cake. Just given Boy his. I hear you wishen him to taste it."

"I don't want the old cake," said Boy stonily.

"Might just eat it my ownself, then," said Isaac.

Gump's face was a puzzle. Plainly the prospect of challenging tall, muscular Isaac dismayed him.

"Here," Isaac tossed him the cake. "Wouldn't nobody want to eat it now, with your spit on it."

Gump crammed the whole slice in his mouth. "I'm going to get you," he mumbled. "You wait and see if I don't."

"I'll wait," said Isaac serenely.

Gump stamped off.

Alone again with Isaac in the fireplace corner, Boy opened her mouth to ask the myriad questions that bothered her. But Isaac had questions of his own. "For true, you know how to read?" he demanded.

"Of course. I already told you that."

"And write? You can do writing too?"

"Yes yes yes—what do you want, proof? I'll give you proof." She drew in the ashes of the hearth. "*I-S-A-A-C*, Isaac; there. That's your name. Anything else you want me to write?"

He pored over the letters. With reverent finger he traced the lines. "For true, that be my name?" he marveled. "My name! Show me how to do it, write my name. Can you show me?"

"Sure," said Boy. "All you have to know is your ABC's.

I'll teach you those, and we'll get you an easy reader—and I'll help you practice—and . . ." Her voice trailed off. She faced him. "I'll teach you if you'll tell me what you know about my mama and daddy." The only way was up now, she reminded herself.

He looked away. "They finely."

So Aunt Jenny had declared. But Boy sensed something held back. She persisted. "Do you know where they are?"

Still he did not meet her eyes. At last, grudgingly, he replied, "Say they taken you pappy Master Isenhour's."

"Where my mother is, you mean? In Freetown," she guessed shrewdly. When he looked surprised, she reminded herself that he knew nothing about Overtha. He couldn't read. He didn't know what that newspaper said. "Took him to Isenhour's," she prompted, "took him there when?"

"Yesterday," he confessed softly, and haltingly he related the horrible details. The slave catchers back in the mountains had run Jeffrey down with their dogs, and they had buried him at Isenhour's on Christmas Eve; her father was dead, killed.

"What did you say his name was?"

"Jeffrey; Yancey's Jeffrey."

"My daddy isn't called Jeffrey."

He couldn't figure that out. "Slave catcher told Pa they kilt Jeffrey, but he boy got away."

"Maybe so, but my daddy sure isn't any Jeffrey."

Isaac's eyes glowed, and she was touched by the sweetness of his smile. "It bout ruined me all this time, thinking how I got to tell you." He shook his head sadly. "Bad Christmas Eve."

"Now, you're sure it's yesterday you're talking about?

Christmas Eve this year. What year?" She watched him closely.

"This year, 1853," and he wrote it with a flourish in the hearthstone dust: *1853*. No mistake about that; 1853 was certainly the dateline of that newspaper.

"Thought you claimed you couldn't write."

"I can't, but I know how to figure some." He boasted that he knew how to count the clock as well; his mother had taught him how. Mistress had learnt his mother to count clock so she would know when to take dinner out to the fields. His Muh knew a lot of things from working in the big house.

"Which big house? The one where Ike got the Christmas presents?"

"That's it. Pa holp Master build the big house fore he ever bring Mistress there to live."

"And you left your mother there?"

"No—not there." His square shoulders sagged, and his good, square hands, trembling, fiddled with the stiff leather thongs of his brogans.

Their master had died the previous winter, he said, and the mistress had been obliged to sell off her property, bits at a time. Isaac's mother, as the least valuable of the slaves, was the first to go. The father and son would likely be put up for auction, together with the house and land, before planting time in the spring.

They had been promised, Isaac and his parents, that they would never be sold separately. But the times were hard, and the mistress had to live somehow, being a widow, and she had been offered a tempting sum for his Muh, who was as good a weaver as ever there was. So she had sold her to get money to live through the winter.

Boy was shocked. "I don't blame you for running away. What a mean, wicked woman!"

No, Isaac denied. She wasn't wicked. She was a good, kind mistress, better than most. It wasn't her fault the master died. But when her goods went up at auction, there was no guarantee that Isaac and his father might not be sold separately. It often happened that way. They talked it over, father and son, and agreed to wait until they had received their Christmas clothing. "And then," said Isaac, "we runned away to look for Muh."

They had hoped to be united with her at Cedar Springs, but the slaves from that plantation had brought the news here, to the Christmas frolic, that she had been sold twice in the same month, because she kept running off, trying to get back to her dear ones. Now she had disappeared, and some said run away again, but some said she had been sold south, and still others said a slave stealer had got her. In any case, it was likely they would never learn anything more about her.

"My Muh, she were a storyteller.' Isaac swallowed. "Any frolics like this my Muh be at, or cornshuckings or lay-by time, folks all time come round begging a story. Tell a story, tell it again, they say." A tear straggled down his cheek.

Respecting his grief, Boy got up and walked across the room to the water bucket. In the cabin's dim light her face swam and leered at her from the water's surface. Demented, that's how she looked. They kept saying she was crazy; they might be right. It was hard to hang on to your wits when you didn't really know who you were. To the people here she was Yancey's boy, an outsider, a bit wacky. But all they went by was her old jeans and short haircut, and her different way of talking.

That newspaper ad scared her, though. It was like somebody knew her better than she knew herself. Who was Overtha, whose description matched Boy's exactly? It had to be an ancestor with that name, probably the one all the girls in their family had been named after for generations.

But what if that ancestor were Boy herself? If she put on a smock, like the little kids here were wearing, and plaited her hair, and she already had a pronged scar on her cheek that looked exactly like a Y brand. . . . Well, she wasn't going to think about it; she would definitely try not to think about it. Inside her skin, she still felt like herself, twentieth-century Boy Yancey.

But then again, she wasn't in the twentieth century. Boy Yancey's mama and daddy weren't even born yet. No matter how much she hated it, she had to think seriously about who she was, or pretended to be. And right at the moment, it was probably safer to be Yancey's crazy slave boy than a runaway slave girl with a price on her head.

"Get you coat and quilt," said Rosalie at her elbow. "We bout to go now."

– 8 –

IN THE CHILDREN'S HOUSE

"**M**e? I'm supposed to go somewhere with you?" Boy asked.

"Chillen's house. You be safe sleeping there." The woman pressed Boy toward the door, where the partygoers in pairs and groups called their goodbyes and drifted away in the night. Ike and Isaac, it seemed, meant to sleep in the field, where Uncle Jim said there was a blind ditch. Several of the men nodded at one another.

Boy looked longingly after them as they filled gourds with live coals from the fireplace and shouldered their bedrolls. Fearful of Ike though she was, she hated to part with Isaac.

"You too little for running off like mens, son." Rosalie interpreted her glance. "Best you keep in the chillen's house long as you can." She led her away to the large cabin where Ike had inquired earlier in the evening.

The stout woman let them in. A draft from the open door whipped up a brief flame in the fireplace, and in its light Rosalie bedded her little girls down on a floor carpeted with sleeping children. Pegged to the walls were several bed frames strung with cords like the one in Uncle

55

Jim's house. Rosalie loosened her clothing and climbed into the only one vacant. Boy stood clasping her quilt forlornly.

"Here, honey, you can sleep here tonight." The mother patted the narrow space beside her. Boy balanced on the very edge, miserable.

Sacking filled with straw served as a thin mattress, and there was a pillow of sorts, also made of sacking but stuffed with some lumpy material, probably cotton. The crisscrossed cording complained when the woman shifted, and the straw mattress whispered. A child on the floor sat up, looked at Boy with round, alarmed eyes and cried out, "Mammy!"

The stout woman said, "Hesh, child. Lie down."

The child continued to stare. "Who that, Mammy?"

"Lie down, I say. Old Raw Head and Bloody Bones going to get you."

The youngster hastily pulled a cover over its head and was still.

Boy unrolled her quilt, removed her shoes, and settled into the rustling bed. Beside her, Rosalie breathed deeply.

The blaze on the hearth died out and the room grew dark and hushed. Occasionally a child whimpered in its sleep. A star glimmered through a crack in the roof. If Boy closed one eye, it disappeared. When she opened both eyes, it beamed down on her again. She tested her sanity playing hide-and-seek with the star. Lost. Found. The star had found her, she thought, but in the wrong century. 1853!

In the movies, when people were caught in a time warp, they jumped into a spaceship and zoomed out of it or built themselves a time machine to escape in. She knew that wasn't ever going to happen here, not in this old-timey valley. She didn't want a time machine, anyway; she wanted Mama and Daddy.

It was awful, not belonging to anyone, not having anybody to care about her. She wanted obscurely to blame her parents for all this, and as her mind drifted, she imagined them sneaking off from camp and hiding somewhere just to tease her. Where the picnic tables and grills used to be, they left this slavery time instead. They weren't ashamed of slavery; they were proud. They let it happen on purpose to teach her a lesson.

"You, Boy, don't run off, Boy!" She heard Daddy's voice calling to her from the hiding place, the way a master spoke to a slave. It wasn't funny; she was furious with them both; it was all their fault. "Don't you call me Boy!" she hollered out.

Rosalie jerked awake in the bed beside her. "Whuh—whuh—?"

"Mammy!" wailed one of the tots.

"Hesh! Old Raw Head . . ."

"Sorry, I had a bad dream," Boy apologized, and Rosalie rubbed her shoulder understandingly.

Somewhere in the cabin a baby began to squall. Rosalie crawled out of the bunk and made her way toward the insistent howls.

Boy wanted to cry too, waa-waa, like that baby, and make her mother come to her. But this was 1853—Mama wasn't even born yet, wouldn't be for years and years. And Overtha's mother couldn't come to her because she was owned by Mr. Isenhour in Freetown. Instinctively Boy touched the scab on her cheek. She understood now why Overtha had been branded; and she understood, too, that she had to go to Freetown. For she must be related to Overtha—and to Overtha's mother.

Will I know who I am when I get to Freetown? she wondered. What if I turn out to be my own great-great-grandmother?

Voices from outside roused her. She was alone in the bed. A window shutter propped slightly open let in the melancholy light of near-dawn. Rosalie sat on the floor by the fire, nursing her baby and murmuring to another woman who held two babies in her lap, feeding at both breasts. On the floor children continued to sleep, but a few now stirred, their slumber broken by morning sounds.

Boy dozed in the grateful comfort of her quilt and would have slept deeply but for an insidious anger that blended in her dream with cooking smells from outside. The cake, she remembered, she had been cheated out of her cake; and she was starving! She came fully awake. She threw off her quilt, slid into her shoes and padded out the door.

At the chimney end of the cabin, under a shed, the woman called Mammy was serving breakfast to a throng of shabbily dressed men and women. Some of them wore sacking thrown shawl-like over their shoulders against the frigid morning. The women in the crowd had on long skirts, and in spite of the bitter cold, many were barefoot. Boy tried not to stare at their terrible feet. They looked like misshapen old boots, thickened, cracked, leathery. Some of the men went barefoot too, but others wore new brass-toed brogans and new full-sleeved shirts.

They were lined up for breakfast, all armed with wooden spoons and trenchers. To each Mammy served a ladleful of hominy swimming in grease, together with a slab of cornbread for sopping up. The breakfasters dipped tin cups into a cauldron of some dark brew that looked but did not smell like coffee. Molasses from a bucket and milk from a tin pitcher were occasionally added to the drink.

Boy stepped up, drawn by hunger. She looked all around for a spoon and trencher to use, but she saw no extras anywhere.

Before the last in line had been served, early finishers queued up again for seconds, and Boy pushed in quickly, lest the morning's breakfast go the way of last night's cake, with everybody getting a share but her.

"You there, Boy," Mammy called to her, "fetch a piggin of water whiles you just standing about."

She didn't care at all for the tone of this fat, bossy woman. But last night had taught her you didn't talk back to the boss. Especially, hungry as she was this morning, if the boss happened to be the cook. She hastened to pick up the squat wooden tub the woman pointed out. "Yes, ma'am! Just tell me where the spigot is."

"Spring's up the hill," Mammy motioned. "Foller that round the cabin."

The path she pointed out, a wide, well-trodden one, turned steeply up an embankment in back of the children's cabin. On the other side of a ridge, running through a ditch from a higher ridge, a log flume fed a ribbon of water into a pool formed by damming up the ditch at its lower end. The pool was paved with river stones and ringed round with fetterbush and ferns.

Boy knelt on a flagged curbing to fill the piggin. One wooden stave longer than the others made a perfect handle for dipping, but it was going to be awkward carrying it back to Mammy. And heavy; a gallon of water weighed what, eight pounds, and the piggin probably held over two gallons. She stood up, hoisted the vessel experimentally and tumbled, piggin and all, into the water.

The basin was shallow, no more than waist-deep, but it contained icy spring water. She struggled to her feet, gasping with shock, and scrambled out onto the curbing before she comprehended that she had not merely lost her balance; she had been shoved in. Dancing on the curbing, hooting and jeering, Gump mocked her watery plight.

"Crazy fool idiot," Boy yelled at him. "Why'd you do a crazy fool stunt like that?"

"You the idiot," he answered her fiercely. "You lucky I never drownded you!"

She was shivering and trying not to cry. "Drown me? Why? What did I ever do to you?"

"They told it was me laid hands on Missy," he spat. "Say it's me that's loony. And they sending me back to Cedar Springs, making me lose my holidays, and frolics, and good eats and all—ain't no frolics in Cedar Springs; they all got to work double on Young Master's infare what's coming up. And you the loony that's to blame."

"Infare?—I don't know what you're talking about. I never told anybody anything; I don't know what you're talking about." Boy's teeth were chattering. "I don't want to get anybody in trouble. If I'm the fault of you losing your holidays, I'm sorry."

"You sorry!" Her apology enraged him. His eyes joggled madly, and he clenched his fist in her face. "Sorry! Sorry just a mule you ride to keep from walken. I'll teach you how to ride sorry!" He yanked off a branch of fetterbush and slapped her across the ear with it. "Giddyap, mule." He seized her by the arm and raised his whip.

Incredibly, the fetterbush at the water's edge rose up and thrust itself against the punisher. Off-balance, Gump staggered on the flagging, clawed the air and splayed backward into the basin. The fetterbush murmured, applauded the show, parted its branches and yielded up—Isaac.

"Oh, Isaac," was all Boy could think to say.

Isaac knelt on the curbing and extended his hand. "Here, Gump." He hauled the soaked fellow from the water. "You better get you some dry clothes on before you head for Cedar Springs," he said mildly. He rolled up his sleeve and began groping for the sunken piggin.

"You—Boy, Isaac—I'll fix you—" the crosseyed boy sputtered.

"Master fix *Gump*, if Gump miss that haywagon," Isaac warned. "Haywagon's all set and fixing to leave." He jerked his head in the direction of the big house. The distant *clink* of harness chains and the hawing of mules confirmed this.

Gump jigged with impotent rage. "You ain't none of us," he shrieked. "You runaways, you and you pappy, and there be a slave catcher glad to know where you hiding. They pay plenty shinplasters for catching runaways." He nodded malevolently. "Might just be a shinplaster in it for me."

"Might," Isaac conceded. He lifted out the piggin brimming with water and set it aside. "If a shinplaster's worth a broke head to you."

The driver's voice, bawling at the mules, diverted

Gump. He flapped his wet sleeves and headed toward the road. "I'm gone fix you," he vowed, departing.

Isaac said to Boy, "You best get on dry clothes, too, fore you start spewing ice." Below the spring, the ground spewed in bristled waves where last night's frost had flowed.

Ground spew, Boy thought vaguely; who said that before? She shivered. "I don't have any dry clothes." Her teeth chattered.

"Mammy give you some outen the chillen's house. Make a regular shirttail boy out of you." Isaac's tone suggested that he himself had surpassed the shirttail stage. He handed over the piggin of water, and when Boy staggered off with it, sloshing, he advised her to carry it on her head. Gamely she tried it, holding the container level with her hands. Her skull hurt and water splashed into her face, and at last he took pity on her.

He swung the piggin onto his own head and moved gracefully down the slope. Isaac could balance the vessel without using his hands at all, and he could turn all the way around under the load and not spill a drop. He grinned, showing off. "Top my head wore plumb out carrying water," he bragged. At the corner of the children's house he lowered the piggin and bent his head to prove it. Sure enough, there was a bare patch on his crown the size of a quarter.

She could not get Gump out of her mind. "That cross-eyed boy," she said, "he scares me."

"Talk. Gump nothen but talkified."

"But he knows you're a runaway slave, you and your daddy too."

He stiffened. "What you think *you* are? Just cause you Yancey's pet boy—"

She hastened to patch that up: "Well, I'm scared of that slave catcher he talked about. You aren't?"

"Plenty scared," he admitted. "They got guns, got whips. Got dogs tear you up, do they catch you." However, he squared his shoulders manfully and said, "Long as they don't catch you, you running free. *Free.*"

An angry voice called out, "Boy! You there, boy!"

She turned. When she looked back, Isaac was no longer there. Somehow, in an eyeblink, he had dissolved.

"Bout as well fetch water myself fore I send a no-count boy. Boy!" Mammy wheeled around the corner of the cabin and brought up short at the soaked figure on the path. "No count," she repeated disgustedly. "Go dry off inside." She lifted the piggin to her head.

"I'm sorry—" Boy began.

Mammy waved dismissal. "Won't so much of you melted in the water that it taste of Yancey."

The cooking shed had been vacated. Down the rutted road men and women tramped toward the woods. They carried axes and mauls across their shoulders, and wedges and coils of rope in their arms, and they sang cheerfully on their way to work.

> *Don't mind working*
> *From sun to sun,*
> *If Massa give me dinner*
> *When the dinner time come.*

The sun had pulled free of dawn clouds that lay on the horizon, and now it shone palely on their backs as they

A Girl Called Boy

crossed a plowed field to the wooded slope where, in this season, they cut timber. The morning chill receded. Already the weather promised one of those astonishing springlike periods that punctuate the North Carolina winter.

> *Old Massa give a pound of meat,*
> *I et it all on Monday;*
> *Then I et lasses all the week*
> *And buttermilk for Sunday.*

The leftover hominy had been dumped into a wooden trough set upon trestles. Boy eyed it wistfully. "Am I too late for breakfast?"

"Horn ain't blowed yet," said Mammy crossly. She poured water from the piggin into her kettle suspended on an iron tripod over hot coals.

The singing came back fainter now.

"Can I have some hominy to carry out where Ike and Isaac are hiding, in the blind ditch?"

Mammy jerked upright. "Hesh that talk round where folks can hear you. Ain't nobody hiding. Get inside like I told you and don't come out no more till I blow." She turned back to her kettle and poked the fire underneath it.

– 9 –

MUSSELING

The children were all up now and their pallets folded and stored beneath the corded beds. Someone had doubled Boy's quilt tidily on the foot of the bunk, Rosalie perhaps, although there was no sign of Rosalie—not her blanket, not her clothing, not herself.

Boy unfolded the cover and shook it out for inspection. There had been a shirt in it, or on it, she remembered. She found it at the corner, a long, gray-striped woolen shirt, faded and mended and quilted with other worn garments into the serviceable patchwork fabric she used for a bedroll. With the blue plastic clip of her ballpoint pen she picked out the coarse stitches and pulled the shirt loose from the quilt.

"Turn your back," she ordered the toddler watching her.

The little girl merely stared.

Boy draped the full garment around herself and managed to wriggle modestly out of her own shirt and jeans. She spread the wet clothing to steam at the fireplace.

The children in the room weren't all toddlers. Many were as old as she. All save the three babies parked in

65

splitwood baskets wore drab striped shirts that fell to their knees. The shirts looked like the uniform of some shabby institution, a girls' orphanage, Boy decided.

Not only girls wore those shirts, she soon discovered, as a circle of children bent over to shoot marbles at a target scratched in the dirt floor. Her startled eyes were favored with the bare innocence of three boy behinds. She blinked and tried to look indifferent.

Rosalie's little girls were engaged with the other toddlers in a game that entailed much running and hiding and squealing. "Peep, Squirrel!" the cry went up, whenever the leader discovered bright eyes peeking from behind a pile of pallets. The captured squirrel had to retire to a cage with other captive squirrels, there to scream with laughter when the next inquisitive one was caught.

Outside, Mammy's horn bawled. "Breakfast!" screamed the children. They scrambled madly for the door, and Boy scrambled too, one of the mob in her striped shirt. It was wide in the shoulders, and the sleeves were queer and bunchy, but at least it was dry and warm, and it gave her a sense of kinship wearing it.

The tallest of the children blocked the door. "Not you littluns," she rebuked the toddlers. "Ain't you turn for breakfast till us is done. Don't y'all never learn that?"

"Me?" said Boy eagerly. "Is it my turn now?"

The tall girl shrugged. "If you think you big enough." She led the line of older children outside.

Boy didn't know how big she was supposed to be to get her turn, but one thing sure, she was hungry enough. She hoped she could think of a way to get some breakfast for Isaac. That might be difficult under Mammy's stern eye.

In the shed, Mammy passed out mussel shells to eat the

hominy with and chunks of hot cornbread. Boy wedged her way up to the trough. Children crowded on both sides of her, shoveling hominy into their mouths and scarcely bothering to chew.

"Slow down, slow down, y'all," Mammy reprimanded. "They's plenty for everbody, no sense in y'all acting like hogs."

They did act like hogs, Boy thought, but she found herself shoving and shoveling with the best of them, and when the rush began for milk, she was not last in the line. The tall girl handed her a tin cup. Mammy poured, and each child was allowed to sweeten his milk with a spoonful of molasses, dispensed by a boy guarding the molasses bucket.

"That's all you get," said he to Boy.

"More, more! You only gave me half a spoonful," she argued. She felt justified in the fib, having missed out on the pink cherry cake of the night before: it was gone forever, that beautiful cake, and not a taste for her. When he ignored her and turned to serve the next in line, she dipped her hand in the molasses bucket and walked away with her fingers in her mouth, well pleased with herself.

After they had eaten, Boy helped the tall girl lower the trough from its trestle to an open space on the ground. They stirred leftover cornbread into hominy and slopped the mixture with milk for the little children. They too were given mussel shells to dip with, but when the smallest ones lost theirs in the mess, they musseled the gruel with cupped hands instead. In the scramble Boy managed to fill her tin cup with the mixture; she carried it around behind the cabin to where she had last seen Isaac.

"Isaac? Are you there?" she called softly into the dense undergrowth.

She parted the bushes and called again. Then she set the cup on the ground and removed from her full sleeve a square of cornbread, still warm, still in one piece. This she placed nicely on a large brown leaf beside the cup. Some hungry animal might get to it first, but without knowing where to find Isaac, she couldn't think of anything else to do.

Later in the morning, fetching more water for Mammy, she checked the cup and found it empty. She picked it up and saw a familiar number scratched on the ground underneath: 1853.

It was as though Isaac had spoken to her, had thanked her in the best way he could manage, knowing that she would understand. She had a friend! She practiced lifting the piggin to her head as he had taught her, and she hummed a rollicking tune she had heard the children singing:

> *Run, chillen, run,*
> *The patterroller get you,*
> *Run, chillen, run. . . .*

Why such threatening words to that jolly music? And what was a patterroller, anyway? She must remember to ask Isaac, her friend. Isaac would know.

Between trips to the spring, the children of the quarter pulled her into first one game and then another, showing off their skills. Some boys taught her to walk on stilts made from trimmed tree limbs. They pitched horseshoes and ran races and shot marbles. They played Antny Over, throwing a hedgeapple as substitute for a ball, and they took turns riding a homemade seesaw balanced over a stump.

But there was work for them to do, too, and two girls named Sally instructed Boy in the politics of chores. When she had to sweep the yard, she could avoid a second assignment from Mammy by sending the broom back with a toddler. The little ones, unlike Boy, delighted in the endless job of fetching water, and they were proud little bearers of the baskets of chips and armloads of firewood that Mammy continually called for.

The two Sallys were named for Old Mistress. Everybody loved Old Mistress, they said: she handed out buttered biscuits on Sunday mornings. It was the high point of the week, the only time they got to eat flour bread.

"Are you two the same age?" Boy asked. The girls pondered the ground. "Well, how old are you?"

Sally One ventured, "Mammy say us bout old enough to tie up our heads."

"Mammy is your mother?"

Doubtfully, "Yeah. . . ."

"She isn't all these little kids' mother, is she?"

A long silence. "Yeah . . . ?"

They explained about the little kids. Some of their mammies were field hands and lived in the quarter, they said; but they weren't allowed to call them Mother. Mother was for white folks. Mammy minded all the chaps and fed them, and they could go off with their real mammies after the day's work was done.

But children like the Sallys didn't have any mammies or pappies that they could remember. Maybe they had been sold off, they said. That happened. Mammy had always watched after them, so far as they knew. Nights when there was a frolic, she took care of all the littlest ones in the quarter.

"She's a babysitter, then," Boy suggested.

Sally Two declared, "Mammy don't sit on no baby. Mammy don't hardly sit no times. Most times she be working."

Just then Mammy appeared in the door of the children's house. "You Sallys there, tend to Possum and Pickle. You, runt," she pointed to Boy, "mind Handful."

The chore that could not be passed down to a toddler had at last caught up with them. Possum and Pickle, it turned out, were the twin babies Boy had seen nursing early that morning. The Sallys set skillfully about their task, but Boy hung back. She had never diapered a baby in her life, and she really did not wish to begin now.

"Where I come from, boys don't have to take care of babies. They don't know how to," she told the Sallys, hoping to establish herself as a superior, though helpless, male.

Sally Two gave her a bland glance. "Everybody know how here."

"Then why doesn't one of the other boys look after Handful, instead of me?"

"I reckon cause Mammy told you to, stead of them."

Boy tried a different approach. "You're both so good at it! Tell you what, suppose I just watch how you do it this morning. Maybe later on I'll get the hang of it."

The Sallys said nothing.

"So what do you think? You tend Handful this morning, and then tomorrow or maybe the next day, I'll take over, all right?"

Again the noncommittal glance from Sally Two. "If Mammy say it be all right," she agreed mildly. "You go ask Mammy."

Boy gave up. No need to raise trouble where at present none existed. She peered into the third basket at a sweetly sleeping, foul-smelling infant. It worked its plump lips, as in a rapturous dream of milk.

"Is Handful his real name?" she asked.

"Basket name," came the answer. "Him's a her—her real name Sally, name after Old Mistis."

Handful wore a necklace made of nettle-root pieces strung together and knotted with a drawstring pouch containing sourbugs, garlic cloves and cooter bones. They were medicine charms, the Sallys said, to prevent fevers and teething pain.

Sally One also wore a necklace charm. Hers was a silver half-dime punched with a hole and threaded with twine. Wearing it protected her from Old Raw Head and Bloody Bones. Even though she had no means of spending it, Sally One was much envied for her coin. She told Boy she had raced everybody to the gate one afternoon last summer and had been the first one to say howdy to Mistis's company. For that, the visitor had awarded her the half-dime.

Handful let out a squawk when Boy opened her sacking diaper, and Boy felt like squawking herself over the disgusting mess. She wiped gingerly at the baby's bottom, and Handful roared.

"Sh-h, sh-h. Be a nice baby," Boy entreated her. "Pickle isn't crying. Why can't you be nice like Pickle?"

Possum and Pickle, model babies, smiled and cooed, but Handful was only too aptly named. She kicked and bellowed and squirmed, while Boy uttered pitiful bleats and made futile dabs at the flailing legs.

"Keep it up, you gaining on her!" Sally Two encouraged, and Sally One said, "Don't quit now—you biggern she is."

"I can't do a thing with her," Boy wailed. "Please tell me what to do."

"Boys," said Sally One.

"All alike, ain't they?" said Sally Two. She seized Handful by both feet and hoisted her free of her diaper. "You a silly chap," she told her. "Who you think you hollering at?" And like magic, the baby's squalling subsided.

Together the Sallys washed her clean and greased her chubby body. All the while they talked to her, and tickled her, and assured her that she was the prettiest girl in the quarter. Handful gurgled and arched with delight.

She was a pretty cute baby, Boy allowed grudgingly, if you could overlook what was folded inside that dirty diaper.

They dipped a gourdful of soft homemade soap from a vat Mammy kept in the cooking shed and carried it up to the spillway below the spring basin, where the women did laundry on Saturday afternoons, and where the girls were now dispatched to wash an accumulation of diapers. Boy swished out Handful's mess with revulsion, using only her fingertips and trying not to look.

When they brought the dipper back to the cooking shed, Mammy looked at the noonday sun and said it was time for dinner.

"Good!" said Boy. "I could eat a cow!"

"Reckon you customed to cow meat at Yancey's," said Mammy.

"Steak is my most favorite of all," Boy agreed. "Oh, I like other things too, fried chicken especially, and ham or turkey for a change. If I didn't have but one choice, though, I'd eat steak every day and not get tired of it."

"I spect not," said Mammy ironically. She handed Boy a bucketful of buttermilk. "Now, you take Handful out to suck her mammy whiles she eating dinner, and tell her I say fill that baby up, for I don't want her hollering hungry all evening, like she done yesterday."

Boy hefted Handful in her basket and the buttermilk pail. "It's too much," she protested. "I can't carry her and the buttermilk both, all the way out to where they're working."

Mammy glanced around, dropped her voice. "Rest at the blind ditch. Watch out for the overseer. He won't mark you mongst the other chaps." Her voice strengthened. "Now go long and no backtalk. Bout time you done your share. Them that don't work, don't eat."

Boy trailed behind the Sallys and a troop of older children carrying the noonday meal to the field hands. Across the meadow they could hear the *thock-thock-thock* of many axes in the woods beyond, and once the warning cry that signaled the felling of a tree.

Who would believe a little baby could be so heavy? Boy's shoulders ached and her back ached, and although she tried to keep up with the others, there came a time when she simply had to set her load down and straighten her shoulders.

"Boy!" The call seemed to come from under her feet. "Over here, quick!" To her amazement, she saw Ike's head poking out of the ground, like the rest of him had been buried there. He beckoned. Drawing closer, she saw that he crouched in a deep drainage ditch that angled across the meadow. A portion of the ditch had been covered over with poles and brush and sod to form a sort of bridge that people and animals and wagons could cross. Isaac's friendly eyes peeped over his father's shoulder as Ike ducked back into hiding.

Boy set her basket and pail down at the edge. "Is this the blind ditch Mammy said—?" she began, but stopped when Ike grabbed her pail and lowered it to his mouth. He began drinking buttermilk in great, hurried gulps.

"Pick the baby up," Isaac whispered.

Wondering, she lifted Handful to her shoulder. The infant protested angrily. "Wa-ah?" Boy mocked her. "Don't you know I eat fussy babies for lunch?" She nuzzled the soft little belly and Handful laughed out loud. It was somehow very satisfying. Maybe she was developing a knack with babies.

At her feet Isaac whisked Handful's basket into the ditch. Underneath, a wooden shingle covered a trencher of cooked peas and a dusty round of ashcake. Hastily he removed the food, shoved the shingle and the blanket in their place and handed back the basket. He drank in turn from the buttermilk pail and returned that to her, its contents noticeably diminished.

"Best you hurry long," Ike warned. "Stay shy the overseer."

She bundled Handful back into her basket and scurried away to catch up with the others.

The overseer rose from his privileged seat on a log as the children arrived at the work site. He was a florid-faced man, with long, fair hair and darker mustaches that imparted a rather fierce look to his broad countenance. He ran his eyes slowly over all the children with the lunch pails but did not seem to single out Boy. "Dinnertime!" he bellowed in the direction of the workers.

Sally One shyly delivered to him his personal dinner pail, and he rewarded her with a juicy chunk of meat from the stew inside. She stuffed it whole into her mouth, chewing lusciously and pointing her chin skyward so as not to lose any of the dripping. Boy looked on enviously. That meat looked so good.

"Dinnertime!" the overseer bawled again. He sat down apart from the laborers to eat his meal.

Rosalie hurried up to Boy, unbuttoning her bodice. "Baby angel, baby dear," she crooned. She cuddled Handful to her breast and Boy brought her a trencherful of peas. No meat enriched the workers' meal, but it smelled good all the same, cooked with glistening chunks of fat. She watched the mother's work-knotted hands roughly musseling peas into her mouth, delicately stroking her baby's cheek. When a man put down a buttermilk pail, Boy hurried to retrieve it and brought it to Rosalie to drink.

"Thanks, son." She appraised Boy with her eyes, commending her. "Say you run away from Yanceys'," and she gestured with her eyes, warning her, "Stay shy the overseer. He got a devil nose for a runaway."

There at the edge of the woods, Boy dropped down beside her and shielded her face from the overseer. The day had fulfilled its earlier promise, and she basked in the warmth of the noonday sun, but more in the warmth of Rosalie. "You have a nice baby," she said inadequately.

The mother smiled her understanding. "Put you thu a crack this morning, did she? Us don't call her Handful for nothing." She gave a fond jounce to the greedy baby, smacking and pulling at her breast.

Handful was Rosalie's eleventh child. She pointed out two teenage workers who were also hers. Only five children were left to her now, she said, the oldest ones sold off one by one, she didn't know where. Her glance lingered on the tallest boy. "He be going soon, likely," she mourned, "grown so big and strong. Ever time trader come, I vow I run off with my chillen somewheres, but ever time they's a basket baby holds me back. I can't run off from my baby. Some way it just go harder losing chillen, older I get." She clasped Handful fiercely to her and rocked back and forth. "They ain't taking this one from me thout they take me too. Us'll run off, us will."

Boy was instantly attentive. Running was of crucial interest to her, she figured. "Where's the best place to run, do you think? Up north?"

"Dunno. Say it be very cold, son, up north."

"But if you ran up north, the Underground Railroad might help you and you would be free. You know the Underground Railroad—you've heard of that?"

The woman shook her head.

"Well, I think it's some white people that helped slaves escape. They gave food and money, things like that."

"I never heared of no white folks ever done that. Maybe somewheres else. Or," she insinuated drolly, "maybe white folks *say* they done that. Round these parts us is the ones has to help 'em and feed 'em and hide 'em when the pattyroll come."

Boy said, remembering the children's song, "Patterroller? When the patterroller comes, did you say?"

"Yeah, pattyroll."

She made a quick guess. "Patrol. Like, a slave patrol."

"Yeah, pattyroll."

"What do they do, this patrol, or pattyroll, or what-you-call-it?"

"Oh, the sorrowfullest things, son. You don't want to hear me name such sorrowful things. You find out for youself, soon enough. Anyhows, dinnertime bout done."

Rosalie laid the now sleeping baby across her lap and rebuttoned her bodice swiftly with those thick, clumsy-looking fingers. She was a short woman, but brawny, with powerful arms, and she had been a field hand all her life. In the growing season, she plowed and ditched and her daily task was no less than a man's. In winter she cut and dressed timber; all through this morning she had chopped and lifted logs right along with the strongest buck in the gang. In addition, she was acknowledged a good breeder, and the master paid good money and brought in superior male slaves to father children by her.

"Handful too," said Rosalie humbly. She scattered kisses over the face of the limp baby in her lap. "Her an outside child."

Boy was shocked. "Your master pays—I never heard of anything so wicked!"

"He ain't wicked!" Rosalie denied indignantly. "He got to make a living, don't he, same as everbody else?" She pointed out the boundaries of the land her master owned. It wasn't like he was a great planter, with more land than he could ride over in a day. What he owned would just about keep his family and eighty head of slaves, and any extra slaves had to be sold off, if he was to buy his children the clothes and such as they needed and educate them.

"Oh, Master thinks big of us'ns," she assured Boy. She jerked a thumb in the overseer's direction. "That one better never lay a whip on one of us'ns. Any whipping they is to be done, Master say, he take care of hisself." In truth, there was very little whipping done by the master, she declared, and then only when the slave deserved it, like for running away.

Carrying Handful back to the quarter, Boy reflected soberly on Rosalie's defense of the master who bred his slaves the way a farmer would breed one prize animal to another. She remembered Isaac's defense of his mistress, a mistress who had sold his own mother away from him. Would Boy too, as a slave, come to believe that an owner had the right to do such cruel things?

The other children raced ahead of her with the empty dinner buckets on sticks over their shoulders. In the distance they resembled the tiny runaway emblems Boy had seen in the newspaper. There were a lot of those emblems in the newspaper, and one was Overtha's, hers. She felt obscurely proud of that, though not sure yet who deserved it. The next newspaper that came out would probably carry emblems for Isaac and his father. They were like medals of honor, she thought, printed evidence that slaves fought back.

Some children, singing and circling in the road, danced toward Boy as she entered the quarter, and with a rush enclosed her.

Run, chillen, run,

they sang slyly, and Boy thought, Bet your sweet life I will.

But how much simpler if only this were a magic circle, and she could wish herself home again.

The ring broke, and the singers danced away, and Boy entered the children's house, subdued. It wasn't circle magic that had brought her here; it was the conjure bird, the freedom bird. She needed that conjure bird to set her free.

WHO BE YOU?

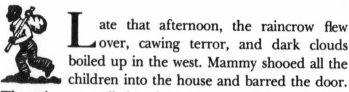

ate that afternoon, the raincrow flew over, cawing terror, and dark clouds boiled up in the west. Mammy shooed all the children into the house and barred the door. The raincrow pulled such storms out of that chubhole there in the sky, she said, and if they weren't careful, the raincrow would reach down their necks and pull the children inside out and backwards.

"Why? Is it a conjure bird, the raincrow?" Boy asked eagerly.

"Hesh that conjure talk," Mammy ordered. "Us-all here's good Christian folks and don't hold with no conjure work."

What about Old Raw Head and Bloody Bones? Boy wanted to argue. What about those charms the babies wore around their necks, and Sally's silver half-dime?

But she was discreet enough to hold her tongue and instead begged to go outside for a minute, only a minute, hoping in some way to invoke the raincrow, just in case. If a conjure bird had worked the evil of her predicament, it could surely unwork it.

Mammy, however, was adamant. Everybody was required to huddle in the middle of the children's cabin, the littlest ones cowering under a quilt, while rain beat the roof. The first moisture squeezed from the crack where the star had winked through the roof last night. A second drop followed, then another, and then a silvery chain drilled a miniscule crater in the hard-packed dirt of the cabin floor.

As rapidly as it had risen, the storm passed over, and Boy raced outside, looking all around for the raincrow. A queer, crystalline green suffused the atmosphere, and she felt both elated and apprehensive in the peculiar twilight. The children burst from the cabin. A final flash of sun poured its energy into them, and they shouted and splattered the puddles in the road.

In the locust grove back of the quarter, mourning doves crooned unseasonably, and Boy's mood plummeted. On summer nights, she often fell asleep listening to the evening calls of mourning doves, which sounded pleasantly sad and peaceful in the shadows outside her bedroom window. Now here, while she was trying not to think of Mama and Daddy, the lullaby reminded her dismally of home and of losing them. She knew it wasn't going to help her any, this brooding.

From the cooking shed Mammy called to Boy, and this evening she welcomed the chore of helping prepare the children's clabber and cornbread. The field hands' meal bubbled in a three-legged cauldron. While Boy set up the long trough, Mammy ladled greens into a trencher and covered it with a shingle.

"You want me to take that out to them?" said Boy.

Mammy turned her back. "You never heard me say nothing."

Boy fled with the food down the road toward the meadow. Behind her, treble voices piped:

> *Run, chillen, run,*
> *The patterroller get you,*
> *Run, chillen, run,*
> *The patterroller get you—*
> *He got a big gun.*

And now from across the open meadow faintly came another tune, as the field hands, their long stint over for the day, raised valiant voices in song on their way home. Dawn to dusk, Boy reflected. A day of grinding labor— and yet they sang!

A rhythmic drumming intruded upon the song. Instinctively she stepped between two cabins, and not a minute too soon. The overseer cantered by on his horse, headed for supper at his cottage, situated a respectful distance up the road from the big house. She certainly wouldn't want him to catch her carrying food out to the field at this hour.

The workers straggled in after him, their song ragged and fading as they made for the cooking shed. Wet clothing clung to their bodies. Boy thought of Ike and Isaac hiding in the drainage ditch through that storm, and as soon as the last hand trudged past, she rushed through the dusk across the open field.

She followed the cart track as best she could, but she had to detour around some standing water that pooled low places in the meadow, and she worried about losing her way in the decaying light.

The storm had drawn behind it a mild, moist air, almost like spring weather. The sky was overcast; no star winked at her tonight. At midday she had crossed the field in company with others, paying little heed to her whereabouts. Alone, she felt unsure of her bearings. Where was that ditch? Tentatively she whistled the children's tune, "Run, chillen, run; the patterroller get you—"

She paused and listened. A dark winged form flapped down in the field close to her. She heard an anguished squeak, more ominous flapping, and then there was silence. Some night bird, out there, devouring its prey. Oh, conjure bird . . .

Tremulously she sang aloud, "Run, chillen, run—"

"The patterroller get you!" Isaac's hoarse voice signaled. How sweetly the melody came to her!

"Isaac!" she called, "Where are you? It's me."

He materialized behind her. "Sh-h-h. We back here in the bresh harbor. Ditch all fulled up after the storm. You best stay off the field track—patterroller run along there most nigh every night."

He led her back to where the woods crowded up to a canebrake. Here the land was marshy and the canes appeared impenetrable, but Isaac parted them like a curtain, and she followed him to the higher ground of the forest. There, in a tiny clearing ringed closely with trees and thatched overhead with brush, log sections lay in orderly rows, like pews. In the gloom of dusk and forest, a cathedral atmosphere exalted the place.

"It's like a church," Boy whispered.

Isaac agreed. "Master don't allow no preaching cept in his church, so they steal the meeting here."

Ike pushed into the arbor. "Hear you coming a mile off," he reprimanded. "If patterroller don't get us, ain't you fault."

The patroller, she learned as Ike and his son shared the contents of the trencher, was in effect a mounted policeman, whose job it was to stop and question any slave outside the quarter after nightfall. Any slave leaving his owner's property had to carry with him written permission from his master; otherwise the slave would be punished, certainly by the patrol, and possibly by the master as well. Even slaves in their cabins were not safe, for the patrol was authorized to enter at any time to make a check.

"There's a path in the canebrake goes up close to the quarter," Isaac said. "I'll walk you back so you don't get lost on the way."

"You're staying out here all night?" Boy looked around. The little clearing, protected though it was, offered cold shelter for wintertime. Fortunately the extreme cold had moderated—or perhaps, like the other slaves, she was growing accustomed to constant exposure.

"We running on to Freetown after good dark. Maybe somebody there know where my Muh been sold to." Isaac spoke calmly, but there was a tremor in his words.

Freetown!

"Oh, take me with you," Boy pleaded. "I want to go there, too."

They bent over the trencher. Ike mumbled through his mouthful, "Are you got folks in Freetown?"

"Yes! I think I do, anyway. Please let me go with you to Freetown."

Ike said, "No, now. I tell you what you want to do. You best leave outen here in a few days' time, go walken up the road broad daylight, cryen, maken out you scape a slave stealer. Anybody these parts show you the way to Bellemont. They take you back in at Bellemont and won't no-body say you lying. Mebbe no whuppen, neither."

She stared at him dumfounded. "Whyever would I want to go to Bellemont?"

"Cause they Yanceys, they you white folks. Better white folks than thesens here."

Boy quavered, "But white folks aren't my folks, not my own people. I want my mother! Don't you know what it's like to want your own family?"

Ike slammed the shingle down on the wooden trencher. It didn't seem to satisfy his rage. He whacked the trencher a second time. "I ain't dragging no pet boy along, no more."

Isaac spoke up. "He come down the mountain pretty good, Pa."

"Whole day long it taken us. Whole day! And the extry mouth to feed!"

"But I can help you this time," said Boy quickly. "I know how to read. There'll be signs on the road that say how far it is and where to turn, and I can read those for us."

"He saying the truth, Pa," Isaac put in. "I seen him reading Master's newspaper. Writ my name in the dirt! Say he can teach me how to do writing and reading for my ownself."

Ike shook his massive head.

Isaac faced her ruefully. He had done his best.

The man said, "You spect to run like that? In you shirttail?"

"Oh! No, sir!" Boy said. "Oh, thank you, sir! I'll just run and put on my jeans. They're dry now. And get my quilt—and I bet Mammy'll fix us some food to carry with us—"

Ike snuffled and snorted. "We ain't waiten. Soon's it be good dark, we goen."

Boy said, on the way to the quarter, "Your father doesn't want me along. So why did he make me come down the mountain with you in the first place?"

Slave catchers were on her trail, Isaac reminded her. They couldn't abandon her to them. And as a potential informer, they dared not leave her behind.

"Why, I didn't know you were running away, or where you were going, or anything about you."

She had sat listening to their plans that first night, he pointed out. They couldn't be sure she wouldn't blab everything, if bad came to worse.

"I was too scared to listen that night," Boy confessed. Tactfully, she refrained from saying she couldn't understand their talk, anyway. That was no longer true, she realized. Her difficulty with the dialect had inexplicably passed. Similarly, she had no trouble in making herself understood by Ike, or Isaac, or Mammy, or Rosalie or the two Sallys—somehow, they now spoke the same language.

Night had fallen. Torches flared in the cooking shed, hospitable, welcoming. Within their light, the voices of children rose in their last romp before bedtime, and the grownups talked quietly as they shared their meal.

Stopping outside the ring of light, she and Isaac made plans for meeting. From the locust grove came the melancholy fluting of a mourning dove. The funeral bird, said Isaac. They would use its cry for their signal.

"Who be you? Who? Who? Who be you?" the dove sobbed, challenging spirits of the dead. Tentatively Boy imitated its doleful questioning.

She was to wait in the children's house until after the

horn blew, when the slaves were bidden to retire. When all grew quiet, she was to follow the plantation road that ran past the overseer's cottage until she came to the high road, nearly a mile away. There the funeral bird's call would unite them. "Run along smart," Isaac warned. "Pa ain't going to study much waiten."

She promised not to dally, and he melted into the darkness.

Boy slipped into the glow of the pitch-pine torches. She took her place among the children clustered around the trough, but she was too excited to eat and soon laid aside her mussel shell.

She went indoors and found a dark corner where she changed into her old jeans and shirt, now dry. She tore the gray shirt into strips and wrapped her feet and legs well, the way Isaac had taught her, and she made her quilt into a compact bedroll.

The mothers of the infants were already busy at the evening tasks assigned them, picking lint from cottonseed, carding. Presently Mammy entered the cabin and set to work spinning cleaned fluff into thread. Boy hastened to enlist her help and explained her plans for joining Isaac and Ike. Mammy heard her through, treadling and humming. When the spindle popped, she removed the cut and commented, "Folks say the road to Freetown is mighty forky. How you spect to foller along the right fork?"

"No problem. There'll be signs. Can you give us some food to take with us, Mammy?"

"No."

"Oh." Boy was disappointed. "I thought I saw some ashcake left over from supper."

"They was some."

"Well, that's all I'm asking for; I didn't mean I wanted you to cook for us. I can take the leftovers, can't I?"

"No," said Mammy.

"Oh, Mammy, please! Why not?"

"Because you ain't going," said Mammy.

"Yes I am!"

"No, you ain't." Mammy reached for another pile of lint. "Light me that grease lamp there and hold it wheres I can see what I'm doing. No! Use two of them long pine needles to light it. Didn't Miz Yancey never learn you nothen? Now hold it wheres I can see—not in my eyes, boy! More to over this way. There. There. Now you stand there and hold it."

For a space Boy stood silently lighting up Mammy's work. Her arm ached and she shifted the shallow dish lamp to her other hand. The liquid grease shifted too, and caused the wick to smoke and smell.

"Mind!" Mammy reproved.

Boy swallowed. "I need to go to Freetown," she said in a controlled voice.

"Well, you ain't."

She said, trying not to sound impertinent, "But you aren't the boss of me."

"Yes, I am," said Mammy. I'm the boss of alls in this here cabin, and I say you ain't going to Freetown nor nowheres else." She added bluntly, "They don't want you, son. You be nothen but a shirttail boy, nothen but a hindrance. Ike said it hisself."

"He changed his mind," Boy declared. "Ike said I could go, and Isaac told me where to meet them."

Mammy snorted. "Hah! Tell you anything to get shut of you. Hold that lamp up higher there."

In the cabin around them children prepared for bed. The two Sallys moved among the smallest of the toddlers, settling them onto their pallets, petting some, scolding others. The oldest of the boys jockeyed one another for the favored spot next to the fire. The mothers of the infants interrupted their evening task to nurse their babies.

The pile of cotton lint steadily dwindled as the treadle pumped and the wheel turned and thread flew up and down the spindle. Mammy dropped her voice and explained that she was acting for Boy's own good. She began reciting the perils of the runaway. Patrollers threatened at night, she said, and slave catchers by day. Boy thought of the coarse shouts back in Ike's cabin, when she and Isaac had cowered in the tater hole; she listened to Mammy's tales of savage dogs and trembled.

The slave stealer was cruelest of all, Mammy whispered. Once you fell into his hands, you were sure to be sold south, far from where you belonged, so that nobody would ever find and reclaim you, not your owner, not your family, not anybody you ever knew.

"Now don't you fret, son," she counseled. "You better off here in the chillen's house where you safe. One these first fine days Bellemont folks come visiting. You run up when you see Miz Yancey and beg her take you home. She be so glad to get you back, you think honey drizzle outen her mouth." On and on Mammy worked. On and on she murmured, telling sad, ancient stories of a brother stolen away, a sister sold, a mother separated from her children.

Boy blinked through her tears and stared at her lamp. The clay dish held a twisted bit of rag laid through the melted grease as a wick. On its protruding lip the flame sputtered, lengthened, released an elegant plume of smoke at its tip. Mammy droned on. The flame wavered, and in its luminous squiggles, Boy seemed to see a tiny figure running, running—running. . . .

When she roused, she was lying on the floor, covered up. The room was dark and she could not immediately think where she was until she heard Mammy snoring on her bunk. Instantly she sat up. Her hand, exploring the floor around her, located a leg of the spinning wheel. Close by she found the lamp, its grease congealed and cold within the shallow basin. Stealthily she bundled up her quilt and crept to the door. By now her eyes knew the darkness, and she inched through the maze of slumbering children without disturbing any.

At the door she paused. In her mind's ear, she imagined the creak of wooden hinges, the rasp of the doorbar that might waken Mammy. She groped her way back to the grease lamp, and scooping out the congealed mass, used it to butter the hinges and doorlatch.

Her precautions rewarded her. The latch glided up and the door swung silently just enough to let her slip through. She softly pulled it closed behind her, looked left and right the length of the quarter and an instant later went flying up the plantation road.

– 11 –

RUNNING FIGURES

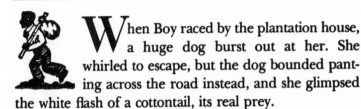When Boy raced by the plantation house, a huge dog burst out at her. She whirled to escape, but the dog bounded panting across the road instead, and she glimpsed the white flash of a cottontail, its real prey.

She proceeded nervously after that, and at the overseer's cottage farther on, slipped from one protective shadow to another, watchful of a single front window that surveyed the road. She imagined that she detected movement in that ominous window.

Sure enough, in the interior, a point of light drifted, retreated, advanced toward her. She crouched in dry weeds and clutched her bedroll. The point of light fluttered and became a candle flame that burned steadily once it was placed on the windowsill. And now a woman's head appeared above the flame, a head disembodied and made ghostly by the fragile flame. The shadowed hollows of her eyes looked straight into Boy's, and her mouth made a fearful black O.

"Oh," Boy breathed, mesmerized. She could not look away from that dreadful skeletal gaze.

The face dissolved into blackness behind the windowglass. Boy leaped from the shallow ditch and fled down the plantation road. She ran until her laboring heart slowed her down. Her quivering legs threatened to give way, but at last reason returned. The thing was nothing but a woman looking out the window, she assured herself. The candle flame had lifted the planes of her face into grotesque relief, that was all. She jogged on until the plantation road entered the high road, as Isaac had told her it would.

If highway it was, and it must be, for the plantation road ended there, it was certainly not a main thoroughfare; the sorry dirt track disappeared in both directions into forbidding twin tunnels of darkness. Boy stood for a moment, wondering in which direction Freetown lay. To her joy, the gypsy moon struggled briefly from behind clouds to illuminate a crude sign that, with a double-headed arrow, pointed the way to Bellemont, and in the opposite direction, Freetown.

All was still. Boy piped the few notes of the funeral bird. Who be you? Who? Calling to the spirit freed at last . . . the freedom bird? Ah! She must remember to ask Isaac about that! She whistled and whistled. The only response came from a mockingbird, who burst into brief, melodious concert, waited courteously, then repeated the aria as though an encore had been called for.

"Oh, shut up," Boy muttered. Mammy's warning drummed in her ears. "Tell you anything to get shut of you."

Had Ike and Isaac gone on without her? They could have, hours ago. She had no idea how long she had slept. On the other hand, if they hadn't much of a start on her, if she hurried, she might catch them up.

Above the dark tunnel that led to Bellemont the moon at last sailed free. She set off with it at her back on the winding, downhill road to Freetown.

Who be you? she called at every turn, and at an unmarked fork in the road, she called again. *Who be you?*

Three faint notes answered her second call. She froze to attention. She whistled. This time the answer came from behind her. She spun around and listened.

"Isaac?" Her whisper was little more than a breath. Nothing. Bolder now, she spoke softly. "Isaac, are you there?"

"YES!" A form leaped from the shadows and grabbed her, and a sinister voice chortled, "Got you!"

She yelped.

"Holler, why don't you?" the overseer jeered. "Go on, holler all you want." Deftly he secured a rope around her wrists and jerked her so that the moon lighted her face for him to peer into. "I been hearing bout you," he gloated. "Yancey's little feller, ain't it? Where was you off to this time of night, boy?" He gave a yank on the rope that burned her wrists. "Don't never mind them other fellers; you'll not see them again, not in your time nor theirs neither." He picked up his rifle from the roadside and hauled her off in the direction of the plantation.

He was a tall man, broad-backed and long-legged. Boy was hard put to keep up with him. Stumbling, scrambling after him, she managed to call out, "Mister, please, I dropped my blanket!"

He glanced back at her and swore, and in that moment of glancing, Boy saw what he did not—two shadowy figures crossing the road ahead of him. "Was it any good?" said the overseer crossly, halting.

"Mm-n?" she mumbled, all her thoughts on those running figures.

He gave her a cuff. "The blanket, stupid. Where did you drop it?"

"Back, back there, where you caught me on the road back there."

"Was it any good, I ast you?"

"Oh yes, it was a good blanket, a real good blanket, all nice and warm and—warm and—all rolled up. . . ."

Grumbling, he led her back. The bedroll lay in middle of the road and the overseer picked it up. He flung it at her in disgust. "Come back for that rag."

At least Ike and Isaac had been given time to escape. Boy panted along behind her captor, her bedroll cradled clumsily in the crooks of her elbows. He strode swiftly, rhythmically, and he had just given the rope between them another brutal yank when suddenly he tripped on something. His legs flew up and he fell flat on his face in the roadway.

Instantly Isaac was there at her side, plucking her arm. "Quick, follow me!" He leaped away.

But her foot caught on the rope that dangled from her wrists, and as Isaac plunged into the underbrush, the overseer regained his footing, recovered his rifle and fired.

Wheeee, sang the bullet past Boy's ear. She actually felt her hair move! He fired twice more into the bushes. "Come outta there, you!" he yelled. "Come out, you hear me?" Angrily he dug Boy's ribs with his toe. "Git on up from there," he groused. "That feller's long gone."

Boy took up her quilt once more. The man stamped in the roadway where a tangle of grapevine wound up around his boots. "Strung that crost the road," he snarled. "Done it a-purpose to trip me up. A man could break his neck, fallen in the dark. Nothen but brutes, them black boogers ain't." He wadded up the vine and flung it in the ditch, and again they set out.

Thoroughly cowed, Boy padded along, hoping at best to spare her smarting wrists from the harsh rope fibers. If he paused to look behind him, she was careful to slow down; when he neared his house, she sped up to match his pace—dancing to his tune, she told herself ironically.

The candle still stood in the window, but a woman inside the house took it and held it aloft, and opened the door for her husband.

"So the elephant caught him a mouse," she remarked, looking Boy over. In the candle's light her face fleshed out, but her pettish mouth and something spiteful in her eyes added no grace to the skeletal face Boy had seen earlier.

"Caught me fifty dollars reward money, that's what I done," the overseer bragged.

"You sure it's not one of the brats from the quarter? Turn your head, boy, so's I can see—" She held the candle closer. "—filthy little scut. Yo, there's a Y on his cheek. It's Yancey's, all right. But they won't be no fifty dollar for thisn. Wasn't but twenty-five offered for the othern, the girl."

"Fifty's what I remember."

"Nah. Fifty for a full hand, maybe, but not for no shirttail boy."

The cottage contained but one room, made two by a divider curtain hanging down the middle. In the half where a double bed stood, the overseer lifted up a square of flooring that covered the dugout underneath the house. He flung Boy's quilt down and motioned her to descend, for his wife refused to let him lock the prisoner in her good clean cupboard. "Bad enough him spreading his lice and fleas and such downcellar."

The cave was barely deep enough for her to stand erect in, and it smelled of damp earth and a yeasty odor that she could not identify. Mushrooms? Overhead the overseer dropped the square of flooring back into place, and Boy listened as he dragged the bed to stand upon it. No hope for getting out of here.

But the candlelight found its way from the bedroom between cracks of the floor, and she saw that her prison was not unfurnished. A row of crocks stood on a plank bench along one wall, and opposite them, two large barrels fitted with spigots. She opened the spigot of one, hoping for a cistern, for she was very thirsty. What poured forth in her cupped hand met her lips pleasantly; rainwater, perhaps? Then she recognized the yeasty scent and the flavor. Beer. A whole barrelful of beer. Yecch! The other barrel contained a fruity liquor that scalded her tongue.

She turned to the row of crocks. Three held sauerkraut. Wax sealed the rims of all the others. She tried scraping around a lid, but it was tedious work, for her nails were broken and her fingers clumsy, and she had scarcely begun the task before the cellar plunged into blackness. Overhead, bedropes creaked as the overseer and his wife retired.

They talked for a while. "Kilt the one that tried to get away," the overseer boasted. Liar, Boy noted. His shot hadn't gone anywhere near Isaac. "Gump told me they was three of 'em, but I only seed two. Kilt one, caught one, not bad." So the crosseyed boy, Gump, had betrayed them!

"The master likely keep the reward for hisself," Boy heard the woman say. "You won't get penny one for catching the boy."

"Master ain't gone know," her husband retorted.

"How you keep him from finding out, I like to know?"

Boy strained to their words. It was her future they were deciding, up there in that bed! She listened to the overseer's scheme for returning Boy to Bellemont under pretext of hauling a load of corn to the mill. He meant to claim that he had captured the little slave near Linney's Mill. Yancey would pay the reward, and by the time he rode back to Linney's, the grain would be ground and loaded and he would drive home with meal in the wagon and fifty dollars in his pocket.

"Spose Miz Yancey tell Master, how you gone splain it then?"

"Miz Yancey ain't gone tell nothen. Master ain't Miz Yancey's kind of folks, that she talks to."

"But word gets around. Twenty-five is a lot of money."

"It were fifty," the man claimed.

"Wasn't but twenty-five," said the woman.

The two fell to disputing, and Boy crept back to the row of crocks. Her ballpoint pen ought to gouge out that wax, she thought. And so it did. The jar contained stewed tomatoes. She drank the juice thirstily and ate a bite of tomato.

-12-

ON THE ROAD TO BELLEMONT

Before the sun had fully risen, they were on their way. Boy rode in the wagon bed among sacks of shelled corn, covered by a tarpaulin. To one of her ankles was shackled a length of chain that weighed more than she did. After jolting along for an hour in this fashion, the overseer allowed her to share the driver's seat up front.

In silence they traveled along some of the worst roads Boy had ever seen, washed out, rutted, unmarked. But for all their disrepair, the roads carried a frequent traffic of wagons and buggies. Horseback riders saluted without slowing down, but wagons and buggies paused and the occupants exchanged greetings and bits of news from town and plantation. Listening, Boy began to understand the talk of crossroads, springs, forges, mills. That was how these people lived. Some of them were, like themselves, headed for Linney's Mill to grind their wheat and corn. Their horses must be shod and tools fashioned at Yancey's Forge. Their bought goods came from the store at Feimster's Crossroads. Their kin lived on the Cedar Springs Road. The place names described their self-sufficient world. The respectful tone people used about it described Bellemont.

Bellemont. She knew it was a grand house, having seen it from the Overlook. The Yanceys must live like kings in the valley. In a house like theirs, there would be good things to eat, even for slaves, perhaps; and Yancey's boy was said to be the mistress's pet. Daydreaming, she imagined Mrs. Yancey saying, "Welcome home, Boy!" (Or even better, "Welcome home, Overtha!" She could become herself once more, a girl—wouldn't that surprise the overseer!)

But suppose they wouldn't take her in at Bellemont? Suppose they said, Oh, no, that's not our little slave, and the overseer carried her back to his house and made her a slave to his wife? With this depressing prospect, she abandoned her fantasy abruptly. If only I had the conjure bird to get me out of this, she thought. How many times already had she longed for the conjure bird!

In the middle of the morning, the overseer unwrapped slabs of bread and cold bacon and began eating. Boy watched his feast until hunger drove her to remind him, "I didn't get any breakfast."

The overseer favored her with a hard look and continued eating. "You'll get your 'lowance at Yanceys'," he said.

To take her mind off food, she tried to invent a story to tell at Bellemont, in case they refused to take her in. But she couldn't think of anything but the truth, and who was going to believe a girl who claimed to be over a hundred years old?

Linney's Mill was a tall, gaunt, weathered structure with

one small window at the top and one small door on the loading platform. It stood at the neck of the valley, where the river entered naturally into a millrace that partially diverted the spout of a modest falls. The wagon bed pulled level with the loading platform. The driver alighted and went inside the mill.

It must be nearly noon, Boy thought. Her stomach felt as if it had missed a dozen noons. Loose siftings whitened the loading platform underneath a chute where bags of meal came down. In one place, the meal dust formed a pyramid; there was probably a double handful there. It would at least be something to eat. She lifted her chains experimentally. Many hammered shackles weighted the intervals, heavy enough lifting for a slave gang, let alone her. But even as she calculated her strength, the overseer came out the door with a Negro man, who began heaving bags of corn from the wagon onto the platform.

The overseer saddled one of his team, unlocked Boy from her chain and boosted her to a seat on the rump of the horse. After a few last instructions to the millhand, he mounted and returned once more to the high road.

There were no further exchanges with passing travelers. Their horse was made to gallop for long stretches, and Boy conjectured that it must be a great distance to wherever it was they were going. The sun had passed overhead before they came to Feimster's Crossroads, where they stopped to rest the horse while the man went inside a shabby little store for refreshment. He allowed Boy to climb down and stretch her cramped legs, but for the short time he was gone, he strapped her wrists to the same hitching post where the horse was tethered.

RANAWAY! RANAWAY!! RANAWAY!!!

The storefront served as bulletin board to the wayfarer, and the familiar symbol of a fleeing figure embellished several broadsides tacked there. Ranaway, LEMONT ... Ranaway, my man EZEKIAL ... For Auction, one lot of likely slaves ... For Hire, ten good Flax Hands ... Ranaway or stolen before Christmas, my Negro girl OVER-THA ... Boy's scalp prickled in fear and confusion.

The overseer came out, picking his teeth. He studied the posters, and his index finger moved laboriously along a line of print. It occurred to Boy that he must be virtually illiterate. When he untied her, the country ham on his breath made her stomach knot, she was so hungry, but she knew it was useless to beg for food. They rode on.

In midafternoon, they came to the first road marker she had seen all day, and they turned in the direction of Bellemont. A few miles along, a second sign, nicely carved, directed them to a handsome entranceway at the foot of a steep hill.

BEL-LE-MONT PLANTATION
James Yancey, Prop.

For nearly a mile they ascended an avenue lined with buttonwood trees, their bare branches woven overhead. At the top of the hill a gravel driveway circled a clipped mound of abelia in front of the brick mansion that Boy recognized at once. It was splendidly porched, pillared, galleried and cupolaed. A small black boy ran from under the high, arched porch to hold the horse.

"Go fetch your master," the overseer ordered.

"Master gone," said the boy.

The overseer swore. "Gone where? Gone calling? Gone hunting? Is your miss gone too?"

From upstairs a woman's voice called out, "Are you

looking for Mr. Yancey? He is in town this week." A woman of middle years came to the gallery railing. She frowned and shaded her eyes against the oblique rays of afternoon sun. "I expect him back late this evening. Do you wish to wait, or may I help you?"

"Well, ma'am, looks like I done you the help instead— caught your little nigger that run away."

"Overtha!" The woman leaned over the railing. "You found Overtha?"

"I don't know what his name is, says he come from here."

"*His* name? LeMont! Why, it's been months—I'd almost given up—wait there, I'll be right down!"

She rushed out to them through the great front door, pulling a black shawl around her shoulders and over her head. For a moment Boy, sliding down from the horse's rump, thought she was about to embrace her, but the woman drew back. "LeMont," she said, "you don't look like yourself somehow, so changed. Wherever did you find him?" she asked the overseer.

The man began a rambling, boastful tale about pursuing the runaway and capturing him near Linney's Mill.

LeMont! Did they actually think she was her brother LeMont? Or his distant ancestor? If she had not been so intimidated, Boy would have felt like giggling.

"Poor boy, so thin," said Mrs. Yancey. "And look at those filthy rags, I wish you would. Go find Harriet and tell her to give you a bath and see if she can find some decent clothes to put on you. I don't believe you've grown much. Maybe some of your old clothes will still fit." Again she addressed the overseer. "You think perhaps he may have been trying to find his way home?"

Boy took one uncertain step. She had no idea where to find Harriet, whoever she might be.

"Go on." Mrs. Yancey waved toward the front door, standing ajar. "Tell Harriet be sure to use tar soap on you; no telling what manner of vermin you've picked up."

Gladly Boy mounted the marble steps of the mansion. She felt confused and puzzled, but happy to be free of the overseer, and she slipped timidly into a wide reception hall. A movement startled her. She cringed, and saw herself cringe in a gilt-framed mirror that hung above a pier table near the door. She stared unbelieving at the dirty, shabby, mirrored creature. There was every reason for Mrs. Yancey not to recognize her, but by what reasoning should she fail to recognize herself? Alien, mistrustful eyes regarded her. Who are you? she thought. *LeMont?* With something like humor, she reminded herself that after all she was still a girl; she hadn't changed that much. She was definitely not her own brother, or his great-great-grandfather!

"LeMont! Praise God, son, you come home!"

The servant hastening toward her ceased welcoming and began scolding as she approached. "Mercy, child, where you been to get so nasty? March yourself out to the kitchen, fore you rub off on Miss Belle's nice things."

The kitchen was housed in a separate building and connected to the mansion by a covered walkway. From the reservoir of a gigantic iron stove, the woman Harriet dipped hot water into a washtub set modestly in back of a woodpile. Boy retired with a piece of gritty, gray, strong-smelling soap into this meager privacy, and while she bathed, Harriet talked. Boy answered her questions as vaguely as she dared.

The master had gone to Freetown several days ago, Harriet said, in the hope of finding LeMont there. Word had come of a branded boy detained in the Freetown jail, and while the master would have delayed the long journey pending actual identification, Miss Belle had persuaded him to go take a look, for the sake of her beloved LeMont.

The nook behind the woodpile was wonderfully cozy. Balanced on stove wood beside her washtub was a tin platter that Harriet kept replenishing with food she had prepared for Miss Belle's own supper. There were slices of roast guinea hen laid over a mound of sage and onion dressing. There were pork chops and mashed potatoes, candied sweet potatoes and corn pudding. There were pickled beets and pickled eggs and pickled watermelon rind, and there were buttered biscuits with damson plum preserves, and peach leather and grape jelly, and there was besides a tin cup that Harriet kept pouring apple cider in to wash it all down with.

Never had food tasted so good. Never had she appreciated a bath so much. In steamy luxury Boy soaked and watched her fingertips wither as she ate, and washed, and soaked and ate. She felt relaxed and dreamy, and even after she had soaped herself all over for the third time, even after she had eaten her fill, she didn't want to give up her plate or get out of that tub.

At last Harriet took the plate and cup away and laid out clean clothes for her to put on. With a poker she lifted Boy's shabby jeans and opened the firechamber of the iron stove.

"Stop!" Boy shouted. She leaped from the tub and grabbed her precious pants before they met the flames. Her ballpoint pen could have been burnt up! And these old clothes were all she had left to remind her of home. "I know they're filthy," she said to Harriet, "but you'll see what a difference it makes after I wash them good."

Harriet grinned. "Well, I'll say washing made *you* look different from any boy I ever seen—oh, Sugar, it don't do no good to cover yourself now, for I seen what I seen!" The kitchen echoed with her peal of laughter.

"Please don't tell," Boy pleaded. "I don't know what will happen to me if you give me away."

"*I* know," said Harriet promptly. "You'd get whipped and maybe sold south. No, Sugar, I'll not tell. You ain't the first to put on britches and run—bout the only chance a girl's got, dressing herself up like a boy. Tell the truth, you do resemble somewhatly to little LeMont. You and him any kin?"

"Mm-n."

"That so? What kin?"

"I think maybe he's my great-great-grandfather."

Again the kitchen rang with Harriet's mirth. "You a little cutup, I see that. Miss Bell going to pet you worse'n she done LeMont."

A bell that hung from the ceiling clanged, and Harriet laid aside the poker. "Dry off and get your clothes on," she told Boy. "That's probly Miss Belle asking for you now." She hurried out to answer the summons. When she came back, she found Boy dressed and buckling square-toed shoes onto her white-stockinged feet.

"Now, if you ain't the very twin of LeMont hisself," she remarked. "Exact same size. Good thing Miss Belle saved them britches."

Mrs. Yancey awaited her in a large, square room where fire glowed in a marble-faced fireplace and heavy russet curtains had already been drawn against the failing light. At this second meeting, she actually did embrace Boy, murmuring, "LeMont, LeMont, why did you run away from me?"

Her face smothered in a drawstring purse pinned at Mrs. Yancey's waist, Boy could not answer. Anyway, what was she supposed to say? In this world so out-of-the-world, her answers had been for the most part wrong. Fortunately Mrs. Yancey seemed not to expect a reply. "Let me look at you," she said. "I don't know what it is makes you look so changed. Just growing up, I guess. Mr. Yancey is going to be very surprised when he gets home!"

Mr. Yancey turned out to be more than surprised when he arrived home long after the supper hour. He had ridden hard for three days and was tired and angered by his futile trip. "Young savage," he said grimly, looking Boy over. "What he wants is a good whipping. That'll teach him to think before he tries running again." He was a solid, stern-faced man with thick gray hair that he now ran his fingers through in disgust.

Mrs. Yancey defended Boy. "I'm convinced he didn't run away this time, sir. If you had spoken as I did, to the one who brought him home, I'm sure you'd agree. Such a low, greedy sort of fellow. I have a notion he enticed the lad for the reward money."

"Then he needs a good lesson about talking to strangers, and I'm the one who's going to give it to him!" Mr. Yancey was still in his riding clothes, and he smacked a heavy boot with his riding crop.

Mrs. Yancey stiffened. "You can't beat a slave under twelve, James! It's against the law."

"Miss Belle, it's against the law for a slave to talk to

strangers. Why do you suppose they wrote the law? To keep slaves from listening to temptation, that's why. Well, I've paddled my own sons many a time, under twelve and over, and they thank me for it now. Law be damned; I'm the master of this plantation. You know as well as I do a master *is* the law on his own ground."

Mrs. Yancey bent her head, and from the drawstring purse at her waist she drew out a tiny, lacy handkerchief and applied it to her eyes. "Sir," she said, "you may have whipped your own sons, but you never whipped your slaves, nor allowed anyone else to do it. It's bad enough that you let them brand him last time. Now look at his poor, scarred cheek and reflect. Are you truly willing to so brutalize your Christian nature?"

The man stamped about the room, tugging at his hair and glaring at Boy, who stood with downcast eyes beside an immense, square carved piano.

"Please, Belle," he said at last, "no tears, please. I'll not whip him; you know it's not my nature. But this boy has got too much rabbit in him to suit me. Now, this is the third time he has run away and the third time we've taken him back with praises and coddling. If he were one of the children in the quarter, I could better understand, but this boy has had the best of clothes and food and care. Why should kindness make him run away, I ask you. What makes him run away?"

Boy asked herself the same question. Standing there in LeMont's shoes and wearing his clothes, it sure would help to know something about the boy she was pretending to be. She guessed that LeMont would have had sense enough to keep his mouth shut. That was certainly what Boy intended to do, at least until Mr. Yancey calmed down.

– 13 –

THE CRY OF THE PEACOCK

What made Yancey's boy run away? No matter how hard she tried, Boy could not imagine an answer that would satisfy the planter or his wife. Fortunately, although both of them did ask her the question more than once in the next few days, they did not expect a reply.

Mr. Yancey had called her ungrateful, but in that he was mistaken. When she stood at her station behind Mrs. Yancey's chair at mealtimes and waited for tasty scraps and tidbits that the mistress passed her from her plate, she often thought of the children in the quarter jostling at their trough and madly musseling to get their share.

The springlike weather of early February had abruptly ended, and there followed weeks of dry, rasping cold. A perpetual glaze of ice rimmed the well. In the drafty children's house, the little ones huddled close to the fireplace and wheezed in the smoky atmosphere and coughed in each other's faces. The laundress wore grease plasters on her hands from one washday to the next. At night, heavy ice on the lake below the house cracked and howled like a wolf. Lying on her cot under the pastry table in the kitchen, Boy felt thankful to be there instead of in the quarter, or worse, outdoors. Clean sheets, a decent mattress, warm blankets—she knew she was lucky to be a house boy.

She deliberately avoided thinking about her parents; it was too painful, and as the weeks passed she found it took an effort to remember their faces exactly. She almost never thought of her luxurious room at home, with its adjoining tiled shower and flush toilet, and she didn't miss TV one single bit. A TV show was pretty feeble stuff, she reflected, when you were struggling to stay afloat in a real-life drama.

Oddly enough, it was her brother whom she missed now, someone to talk to. Often she thought of him and wished they could be together. Even if he did act rotten sometimes, LeMont was fun to talk to. In fact, in a queer way, she did talk to him, inside her head.

"Told you so," LeMont taunted. "You bragged they couldn't make you be a slave."

"I could run away if I wanted to."

"No, you couldn't. They'd sic the dogs on you. They'd catch you and put you in jail. You wouldn't even know how to run away, cause you never went anywhere in your life except on wheels."

In their imaginary conversations, he talked just as snotty as he did in real life, and as in real life, what he said carried enough truth in it to aggravate her.

She would just show LeMont, one of these days. Not right now, of course. The weather was too cold for running right now, but later on, when it got warmer, and when the life at Bellemont no longer amused her, then she would take off for Freetown; she would look for Overtha's mother. Unless, in the meantime, she found the conjure bird, or the conjure bird found her.

Harriet had given her a large tin box to use for her things, and at the bottom of this Boy folded away her discarded jeans and shirt. All the household help wore suitable clothing, but Boy dressed a little better than the others, and more or less grandly in accordance with the occasion. On an ordinary day at Bellemont, she wore plain lowell-cloth shirts with her kersey knee-pants, but for making calls, she put on a ruffled linen shirt with a Byron collar and a short, embroidered jacket and sometimes gloves.

"Oh, you fell into your luck when you fell to Miss Belle," Harriet told her. "I can't figure how come LeMont to run off from here, when us got the finest place you can get, here on Bellemont. I spect you preciate that, where you come from."

Something condescending about the cook's demeanor reminded Boy of her brother. "Where I come from, it's better," she snapped.

"Sugar, I ain't talking *bigger.* Master bought me out of South Carolina, and I can tell you about bigger you'll never have the first notion of. What I mean is, Yanceys is good folks, treat you like they own chirren, bettern you own mammy and pappy."

"*Bull*oney!" said Boy. "Nobody ever treated me better than my mama and daddy." But Harriet's steely stare made her regret her imprudence. After all, the woman had befriended her, and as custodian of her secret, it would not do to alienate her. "The Yanceys aren't one bit kinder than you are, Harriet," she amended hastily. "Look

Guest Meal Authorization

Date:_____
Bill to: _____
Phone: _____
Charge Acct : _____
Meal Type: _____
Price per meal: _____
No. of guests: _____

_____
Authorized by

_____
Cashier

how good you've been to me. I'd rather have you for a mama than Mrs. Yancey."

Harriet sniffed wisely. "It don't pay to bad-mouth the cook, do it?" She appeared mollified, however, and Boy could only hope that her impertinence would not prove costly later on.

Besides Harriet, three maids served the household, and when she assessed the chores they had to do against her own, Boy at once saw the advantages of being a boy. To the maids fell the revolting job of emptying the chamber-pots each morning. They emptied ashes from the fire-places too and swabbed out the chimneys and polished the fireplace fittings and kept fires going in all the rooms. They had to carry jugs of cold water for the washstands and water pitchers and jugs of hot water for the family's baths. They had also to clean the house and keep the family's attire pressed and in good repair. They washed and ironed and sewed and knitted, and when they had free time they did their own laundry plus that of Boy and the menservants.

Boy's work was largely ceremonial. She accompanied Mrs. Yancey wherever she went, to open doors and gates for her, and windows when she needed a breath of fresh air. She carried Miss Belle's basket of keys for her, and fetched her shawl, if one was wanted.

At table she kept the master's cup filled from the bowl of sillabub on the sideboard. She also stood prepared to fan away flies with a handful of feathers shed by the arrogant peacocks that paced the grounds. Mrs. Yancey raised peacocks for their plumage and because she admired their regal stalking, but Boy hated them; she had the task of cleaning the porch of their pearly, marbled droppings that resembled eyeballs. She hated the ghastly calls the birds uttered. "Help!" they screamed. "Help!"

In the elegant setting of Bellemont, Mrs. Yancey could almost be described as mousy. She was a small woman, with gray strands in her smooth brown hair, and she wore dresses of either gray or brown, for she believed that mature women should attire themselves modestly. Plantation life required her to call on her neighbors and to be called upon by them in turn; driving out occupied many of her afternoons, with Boy sitting in ruffled finery upon the carriage seat beside the driver.

In the mornings Mrs. Yancey wrote letters to her children and played the piano and talked to Boy. She did not often complain, but Boy guessed that she might have been happier living in a city, for she often spoke with nostalgia of her girlhood in Raleigh. Her daughter was there now, attending St. Mary's, and her sons went to the university in Chapel Hill.

"Young Missy is learning French," she told Boy one morning after she had received a letter from Raleigh.

"Yes'm," said Boy obediently.

The letter seemed to unsettle Mrs. Yancey. She played French tunes on the piano and sang "Frère Jacques." She took out a grammar book from the glass-and-walnut bookcase in the library and practiced conjugating irregular French verbs. She was sentimental about the French she had studied as a young girl, and it was she who had given the plantation its name.

"People pronounce it *Belmont*," she told Boy, "but the French would say *Bel-le-mont*. Do you hear the difference? It's really three words, *Bel le Mont*."

"Yes'm," said Boy.

"It means 'pretty mountain' in French. When I first came here as a bride, Mr. Yancey wanted to build on the lake, but I said to Mr. Yancey, 'A house would look so nice sitting on that pretty hill,' and he located it there to please me. Belle's pretty hill, he used to say, thinking it flattery. Fancy! *Bel-le-mont* sounds so much more . . . French."

"Yes'm," said Boy.

Sometimes she felt sorry for Mrs. Yancey, isolated in her mansion. Bellemont was the largest plantation for miles around, and the few neighbors Mrs. Yancey called upon stimulated her mostly to irritation.

"Idiotic woman!" she would say, returning from an afternoon's outing. "She thinks of nothing more than fashion and gossip. I warrant she never looks past the bonnetmaker's advertisement, if indeed the poor simpleton can read at all."

Mrs. Yancey for her part read the Freetown *Chronicle* every Saturday morning. Mr. Yancey rode to the Feimster's Crossroads store on Friday afternoon to buy the weekly publication, and it was his practice to spend that evening reading in the large, square room designated as the library. When he had done with it, he turned it over to his wife, and after she had finished with the single folded sheet, it was burned in the fireplace.

Despite her diligent study, Mrs. Yancey seemed to Boy not much more learned than her neighbors. The tinkling melodies she executed on the piano were all played from memory, and Boy, sitting on the floor at her feet, would frequently fall asleep, lulled by the simple tunes. The woman's conversation dealt mainly with the weather and the upkeep of her house. She talked about her children at such length that Boy came to feel she had known them all her life, but she understood from the beginning what was expected of her in a conversation. Her function was merely to agree with what the mistress said. Her opinions were of no interest to Mrs. Yancey; indeed, that good lady lived secure in the belief that her slaves were incapable of thought and feeling.

"LeMont is my little lapdog," said she to her husband. "If there isn't anything for him to do, he just curls up and goes to sleep. Don't you, Poochie?" She patted Boy's head affectionately.

Boy grinned. "Yes'm."

It was impossible not to like Mrs. Yancey, for at Bellemont, slaves were treated (they said so themselves) like family. Medicine was provided for the sick, and in dire cases, the Yanceys' own doctor examined the afflicted. Special treats were sent down from the mansion for holidays, and frolics were permitted for occasions like the Fourth of July and cornshuckings.

If a slave did his work properly and in good spirit, Mrs. Yancey would write out a pass that allowed him to visit a neighboring farm on Sunday, the only day of rest. One of Boy's Saturday duties was to deliver the pass to the slave who requested it. She was a welcome visitor in the quarter, for she often brought with her a handful of raisins as a treat.

"LeMont! Here come LeMont!" The children would tumble out of their cabin at first sight of her, and after the sweets had been shared around, they would finger and admire her fine clothes and beseech her to tell them what it was like inside the big house. "Say about the clothes they got for bed," they would urge, for Boy had described Mrs.

Yancey's peignoir to them, and her account of Master in his nightshirt and nightcap was so irresistibly funny that she had to tell them the story over and over.

She told them about Mrs. Yancey's pet mockingbird that she kept in a cage. She attempted to explain what a piano was and described the miracles of clock and mirror. Once she took a turkey feather, and dipping it in imaginary ink, traced the words of a pass the mistress had given her to deliver. They goggled over the strange process called writing. They listened awestruck as she read aloud the magic words:

> James has leave to pass and repass from my
> plantation to Mr. Redmons until 12 oclock Sun-
> day night March 9, 1854. Belle Yancey.

"Where it say Belle?" asked a little girl named Belle, and Boy showed her the squiggles that stood for her name. Two girls in the children's house were called Belle, and one of the new babies, James, after the master. There was as well a handsome young fellow in the blacksmith shop named LeMont, for names of the master and mistress, their children and even their plantation were popular with the slaves at Bellemont.

Mrs. Yancey kept all her writing materials in a cherrywood lap desk in the library. To her children she wrote generous letters, filling page after page with her pointed, prodigal script; but slave passes she inscribed on grudging strips of letter paper, frugally trimmed so that no blank paper beneath her signature could be used for an illegal purpose. The leftover clippings she replaced inside the desk, which she was always careful to lock.

Boy enjoyed her importance as handler of Mrs. Yancey's basket of keys. She knew firsthand all the wonders hidden inside those locked cabinets and doors. She told the quarter's children about the padlocked smokehouse, hung to the very top with hams and bacon, and about the kitchen safe, where white flour and sugar were secured. She described the brooches and rings and necklaces locked separately in velvet compartments of a jewel box locked inside a drawer locked inside Mrs. Yancey's high mahogany wardrobe.

The children listened enchanted, as they would to tales of fairyland. Few of them would be privileged to witness such glories in their lifetime.

For a while her exalted position sustained Boy. She fattened on ham and biscuits and strutted around in her fine clothing until Mrs. Yancey began teasing her about being a regular little peacock. (Help! A peacock screamed in Boy's mind. Help! Help!) She thought remorsefully of Freetown and of Overtha's mother. What was she waiting for? She could run away any time now. Winter was over.

Harriet challenged her one day, unexpectedly reading her mind. "You not still thinking bout running away?"

"Away from Miss Belle?" Boy tried to sound shocked. "Why, she's like a mother to me; I'd be a fool to leave Bellemont."

In a way, that was true. Where else, as a slave, could she improve on her life? What she really needed to escape was the nineteenth century! That would require more than running away—that would take magic.

She tested the idea on Harriet. "Do you know how to work a conjure?"

Harriet turned on her in outrage. "Miss Belle better not never hear such talk as that outta you. This here's a good Christian family, if you don't know that by now."

"Oh, I know, I know." At Bellemont, all the house servants had to attend the Yanceys' church on Sunday, and it made Boy want to scream. They had to sit in a gallery at the back of the church and keep quiet: they couldn't even sing, and after the white congregation had been dismissed, they had to stay and listen to the same humiliating sermon, Sunday after Sunday. Mind your master, the preacher warned them. Don't lie; don't steal chickens; don't steal supplies from the kitchen; work hard; a good slave may hope for reward in heaven. On Sundays, Boy envied the field hands their option of relaxing in the quarter. She felt as if she were being brainwashed in that church.

The locked bookcase in the library began to tantalize her, for she could look at the rows of books behind glass doors without being able to get at them. She wondered why she cared. The titles were dull: Grantham's *Essays;* Miller's *Meditations; Sonnets for a Dear, Departed Friend;* and a whole shelf of sermons by the Reverend Thomas W. Ledbetter, who was Mrs. Yancey's own father.

A blue-backed text tucked between two leather-bound volumes attracted her interest: *The Infant's Speller.* Its faded buckram and ordinary lettering contrasted with the tooled, gold-stamped spines of lordlier volumes. Having noted it there, she returned to look again, and for some reason she did not comprehend, to yearn for it. One day, when Mrs. Yancey unlocked the case to shelve a book of poems received from her daughter, Boy asked to look at the blue-backed speller.

"Oh, no!" Mrs. Yancey's voice was severe. As mistress, she dispensed favors through her own largesse, and perhaps the boldness of the request startled her. She relocked the glass door with a troubled face. "Master believes it was this"—she indicated the speller—"this little learning that spoiled you, LeMont, and made you want to run away. So I mustn't teach you your letters ever again."

Boy hung her head, feeling inexplicably ashamed, and the lady continued sorrowfully. "Master says the next time you run away, he'll put you in his pocket. You understand what that means, don't you?"

Boy nodded. She knew all too well, from listening to the people in the quarter: the unruly slave sold south and the money from the sale pocketed.

"It was very wrong of me, for I knew it was illegal to teach a slave to read and write." Mrs. Yancey sighed. "Now, of course, I see the wisdom of the law—too late, alas, as wrongdoers inevitably learn to their dismay. But answer me truly, LeMont, have you not also learnt your lesson?"

"Yes'm," said Boy.

"It could not have been a happy experience, living in the woods out there like an animal and never knowing where your next meal would be found. Surely by now you see how fortunate you are to have a good master who shelters you and gives you food and clothing and everything else you need?"

"Yes'm."

Boy felt drowsy. Often when Mrs. Yancey talked like this to her, she could hardly keep her eyes open. Her mistress meant well, but when she asked you a question, the answer she expected, the answer you *had* to give, in this life, was Yes'm. You could do that in your sleep.

Lately, however, because napping in the daytime prevented her sleeping soundly, Boy found herself waking at night and thinking No! No! No! At those times, between waking and sleeping, she wondered if she were saying No to her mistress or to Overtha's mother.

– 14 –

LAY-BY TIME

"S-st! Son!" A desperate whisper penetrated the wall of cedars that screened the privies. When Boy stepped back to see who was calling her, a hand beckoned her to the women's toilet.

In the dim interior of the stinking little building, a cadaverous creature croaked, "Get me something to eat, son. I ain't et nothen for a week." A sunken-eyed woman, garbed in torn, baggy trousers, clutched her arm.

Boy had been on her way to the children's house with a dose of turpentine and sugar for a baby with the croup. Even now, well into June, adults were still hacking and the children's noses were running, aftereffects of the late spring's wretched weather. Daily through April, Mrs. Yancey had dispatched Boy with blue mass, calomel and castor oil for the sufferers. Today she carried with her as well five teacakes still warm from Harriet's oven and set aside by Boy for treating the little ones in the quarter. Without a word, she handed these over to the woman in the trousers and watched her cram them into her mouth.

"Lord bless you," the woman mumbled. "Oh, son, Lord keep you forever," and she looked prayerfully at the ceiling of the privy.

"Wait here," Boy told her. "I've got to carry this medicine down to the children's cabin. Mammy will take you in there, if it's safe, and give you food. I'll come back and get you."

She returned directly with a blue-checkered shift and Mammy's "fooler." The fooler was nothing more than a huge, cotton-filled cushion with strings for tying it over the stomach like an apron. She helped the trembling woman fasten it in place and slipped the shift over the ragged trousers. "Hold on to my arm," she directed. "Lean back and walk like this." She demonstrated the waddle of a pregnant woman. Together they made their way to the children's cabin.

The children's house at Bellemont was a long, two-room structure with stick-and-mud chimneys angling outward from either end. In the larger room the children dwelt; the other room served nursing and laboring women for lying-in.

In the lying-in section, Boy helped her frail companion onto a one-legged bed built solidly into a corner of the room and made private with quilts that hung around it, strung from the rafters. The cabin mammy appeared with a steaming trencherful of greasy cornmeal pudding, fiery with peppers and onions.

"Eat this kush-kush," Mammy said to the woman. "Eat it slow, and do it set well, you can eat you some more bout dinnertime. If patterroller come poking round here, commence to twisting and moaning. Do he go looking inside the quilt at you, thow you arms up sharp and holler, like you birthing." Mammy flung her own arms up for example and observed with satisfaction, "Mens always scared of birthing."

Runaways were frequent, now that the weather had settled and the nights warmed up. It was not the first time Boy had carried Mammy's fooler up to the privies, and she had grown expert in her role. "Mistress will go calling after dinner," she told the woman confidentially. This latest runaway, traveling in a man's clothing, both excited and disturbed her. She wanted to help her—no, she wanted to *be* her! "I'll come tell you what I hear when we get back."

House servants and drivers were the news source for the quarter, and information and gossip overheard in the carriage or at table were swiftly passed down the line. Boy and the other household help were not supposed to socialize with slaves in the quarter, but through unspoken bond, one or another of them always managed to slip out back to report.

"Bless you, son," the woman told her again, looking heavenward. "Lord bless you too, Sister Mammy, for that good kush." She smacked her lips. "Taste just like good old-timey kush-kush that come from over the water."

By the time Boy returned, the woman had distinctly revived. She was out of bed and pacing the cabin. In the Bellemont turban and checkered shift, she resembled other women of the quarter, and the fooler distorted her slight figure wonderfully. She came at once to Boy, trailing a bevy of children. They had begun calling her Lookup, from the characteristic skyward cast of her eyes. Nobody in the quarter asked the fugitive's real name. It was better not to know.

"They're looking for a horse thief, not you," Boy told her. "They think it's the preacher! Nobody's talking about runaways right now."

"Thanks, son." Lookup put a grateful arm around her neck.

"You don't have to thank me. I know how it is."

The woman regarded her closely. "You've run." She tightened the arm around Boy's neck. "If you've run once, you'll run again."

It was almost as if she had pinned a medal on her.

Boy felt drawn to Lookup, but jealous too. The children had not come running to her when she entered the cabin the way they usually did. Instead they tagged after Lookup, and it was easy to see why. Walking the floor and waving her arms dramatically, Lookup held them spellbound with a story. Boy unhooked a toddler clinging to Lookup's skirt and sat down with the youngster to listen.

* * *

"There was a lame fellow walk in a blacksmith shop one day," Lookup said, "wearing a copperas cap and a copperas shirt and copperas britches. Say to the blacksmith, 'My feets sore. Make me a pair of shoes.'

"Blacksmith hammering a horseshoe, *clang, clang, clang*, never look up, say, "I'm not a shoemaker, boy; I'm a blacksmith.'

"Lightning run through the shop—*zing*—like that; course the blacksmith think it just a big spark like all time is jumping off the anvil; then he hear it thunder and he say, 'Oh, it be fixing to storm, boy.'

"Lightning *zing!*—like that—and the fellow say like thunder, 'Who you calling boy?'

"The blacksmith look quick and see it's the devil! When he taken off that copperas cap, horns poke out his hair, ah ha! Aha! 'Scuse me, sir,' say the blacksmith, 'what I mean is, I don't know how to make no shoes, cause I'm just a blacksmith, but if you go next door, there's a shoemaker will make you a pair of shoes, good pair of shoes, make you the finest shoes you ever wear.'

" 'No!' says the devil, 'I want you to make my shoes, and make them fast.' and he stuck out his foot for the blacksmith to measure. You know what that devil got? Hoofs stead of feets! Little trippy-trotty hoofs like a goat got.

"Well, you be sure the blacksmith get busy and measure his feets and pound out some little horseshoes fasts he can, *clang, clang, clang,* and he took some lo-o-ong horseshoe nails and he shoed that devil, yes sir, he nailed on them shoes with them long horseshoe nails, and he trimmed his hoofs, and the devil say, 'That's more like it,' and he prance out of the shop proud, wearing them little horseshoes.

"Well, the devil traveled a while and his feets got lamer and lamer, cause those horseshoe nails was way too long and they cut into him—whooo-ee! that devil hurting—and by-and-by he come back to the blacksmith and he say, 'These here shoes hurt me; take them off.'

"Blacksmith say, 'Truth is, sir, ever since I shoed you I got bad luck, and Master told me not have nothing more to do with you.'

"Devil say, 'Oh, the devil take your master.'

" 'You mighty welcome to him,' blacksmith say, 'but that still don't take away my bad luck.'

"The devil, his feets hurting so bad, he say if the blacksmith pull off them shoes he will pull off his bad luck. So the blacksmith pull off the horseshoes and nail 'em up over his door; and the devil left out of there and never come back.

"And that's the reason people hang up a horseshoe over their door ever since that time."

* * *

Silence, like that in a theater when the curtain falls, followed Lookup's story. Then, "Tell it again," begged a little girl.

Boy clapped her hands. "You ought to go on the stage!" she exclaimed. "Where did you learn to tell a story like that?"

"From my old Muh," said Lookup. "She got it from her Muh. That's how I learnt everthing I know."

"Tell us another story," said a boy.

Lookup winked at Boy. "Long time ago there was a girl set a trap for Old Raw Head and Bloody Bones," she began. . . .

Lay-by time came to Bellemont. Spring plowing and planting were over, and the crop had outstripped the weeds. Cultivation ceased, and the growing season idled in its cycle, awaiting harvest. When the evening bell rang, slaves were supposed to retire to rest up for the next day's labors, but in lay-by time, as at holidays, there was some relaxing of the rule. In this benevolent interlude, there was time for a frolic, for romance.

On a balmy night late in June, Boy stole out of the big house, ostensibly to visit the privy, but in fact to carry news to the quarter. Both of the district patrollers were bedridden with the summer flux—good news for Lookup. Also, old Mr. Redmon, of Redmon Springs, had died—bad news for the others. Death inevitably meant change. Three of the Bellemont slaves had wives belonging to Mr. Redmon, and one, a husband. What would happen to those dear ones now?

In a dim cabin near the end of the long double row they gathered to speculate and to pray. LeMont, the handsome young blacksmith, withdrew to a corner and began to weep, for only last week, in a secret ceremony, he had married Mr. Redmon's housemaid, Delilah, and the expectation of losing his beloved shattered him.

Boy slipped to his side. "Don't cry, LeMont. Mr. Yancey's a good master. He'll buy your wife when they divide the estate, I know he will."

The man shook his head. "He won't. Master told me I can't marry Delilah. He say too many married outside already, say plenty girls good enough for me here on his place. You know Master be strict about a stole wedding."

At moments of crisis like this, Boy longed to share the hope she alone knew about. Be strong. Hang in there, she wanted to tell LeMont. Freedom is on the way! But she dared not speak out, when for all she knew, LeMont might be dead and Delilah married to somebody else by the time the slaves were freed. What good were Lincoln and liberty, far in the future, if your life was at stake right now?

"LeMont and Delilah jumped the broomstick here last week," she explained to Lookup, who joined her at LeMont's side. "I wish you could see the nice wedding ring he made for her out of a horseshoe nail."

She began to tell what a lovely wedding it had been, thinking to comfort the desolate young man. She told Lookup how pretty Delilah was, with grapevines sewed in her skirt like a stylish lady's hoops, and how sweet, with fragrant Carolina allspice pinned in her hair—

"Oh, Delilah!" sobbed Lemont.

Lookup took both his hands in hers and murmured to him. Her face looked drawn and hurt, as though she understood too well what he suffered.

Poor LeMont, Boy thought. He and Delilah loved each other. Their love was real, but everything about their romance was makeshift, just because they were slaves. The wedding ring, the dress—even their solemn stepping across a broomstick was nothing but a ritual slaves had to patch together because, for them, a licensed marriage was unlawful.

"Unfair! Unfair!" Boy wanted to scream it out, so somebody would hear and help. But who was there to listen?

"Lord, listen to your children," Lookup implored.

The others gathered around her. "Have mercy, Lord."

"Show them the way out of hurtful Egypt," Lookup prayed.

"Yes, Lord."

"Please, Jesus."

"Thank you, Jesus!"

Fervently Lookup prayed, for Delilah and LeMont, and for the other couples threatened by the untimely death of Mr. Redmon. Presently the praying turned into preaching, although no clear signal ended the praying or began the sermon. The husky voice intensified, and the listeners drew near so Lookup need not raise her voice. Two men ran out to the cooking shed and brought back a great round pot, which they turned upside down over a hole scooped in the dirt floor, to trap the sound of the preaching.

"When them Egypt slaves starved in the wilderness, God stuck biscuit all over the yucca, and sillybug poured out of a rock!" Lookup whispered into the cavity, and her words resounded like the echo in a well, muted, but changed and awesome. "Don't be afraid. They's help out there."

It seemed to Boy that Lookup spoke directly to her. She thought of the time Isaac brought her the gourd of water when she was so thirsty but too stubborn to ask for a drink. Sillabub from a rock, if you cared to look at it in that way. There really was help out there!

"And when the slave catcher run them up against the Red River, didn't God lead them through and throw the hound dogs off the trail?"

The memory of that icy stream Ike made them wade, with snow all around, made Boy shiver, even now in summer. She wasn't sure she wanted that kind of help.

One of the listeners objected, too. "Might be them slaves was bad off in Egypt, but here at Bellemont, Master give us biscuit ever Sunday and a good dram when they come cornshuckins and log rollins."

"You're right, brother," Lookup conceded. "You seen enough runaways to know Freedom is hard. But oh my brothers, oh my sisters, Freedom is so good!"

Boy crawled into her cot under the pastry table that night, knowing she would not sleep. Lookup's sermon had made her realize she must choose between Freetown and Bellemont. Too often lately she had put Overtha's mother out of her mind, though through the months she had never forgotten there was someone who belonged to her in Freetown, somebody who cared about her. So what was holding her back?

Mrs. Yancey cared for her, too, she argued. Didn't she

owe loyalty to her mistress? After all, gentle Mrs. Yancey didn't invent slavery. As she pointed out when Boy asked her for the blue-backed speller, it was the law. You were supposed to obey the law, weren't you?

Boy shifted uncomfortably on her cot. She wouldn't like to confess such a thing to her brother LeMont, of course, but there were actually some things about slavery that didn't bother her at all—having her food and shelter provided, for instance, and feeling secure, every part of her life decided by someone else.

She knew she had gotten mentally lazy; she had quit thinking for herself. That made her ashamed. What had become of her pride? Vain enough she still was, preening in her fine clothes and lording it over slaves in the quarter. Yet she was no less a slave than they.

(Help! the peacock in her cried out.)

Her head began to hum with plotting. What if she ran now?

They'll track you down and catch you, said her brother.

But Freedom is so good, Lookup promised.

There's noplace you can go, said LeMont.

I can go to Freetown, Boy answered him. Her heart swelled. She had folks in Freetown. Her people would help her.

She reached for the tin box that held her clothing. She shrugged out of her nightshirt and slid into the ragged old jeans and shirt. Under the cot she located her square-toed shoes, shoes fine enough for a gentleman, and she wrapped them in the good, warm blanket spread over her cot. Her bare feet made no sound when she crept past the cubicle off the kitchen where Harriet and her husband slept. She found Harriet's grease bucket on the stove shelf and dipped her fingers into the fat. When she had buttered the iron hinges and bolt, she slipped silently out of the kitchen and pulled the door shut behind her.

Outside she paused. Between the shadow of the kitchen stoop and some distant, looming trees lay an open stretch of road that she must cross to reach a path in the woods that she had learned about. On that path she could run for miles, for it paralleled the high road.

The road glared in the moonlight. Black shadows menaced. A slight noise behind her set her heart to pumping: go! Her fleeing figure traversed the road and plunged into the woods beyond. In another moment, another figure, a larger figure, pursued her and entered the woods at the same place.

-15-

GET GOING

Boy's bold rush toward freedom landed her on a rock that jabbed her instep. She stumbled into a low branch that knocked the breath out of her. Spurge-nettle stung her bare feet, and when she blundered into skeins of twining supplejack, she halted on the path, whimpering.

The familiar hardships of flight had dimmed in her memory during the comfortable months at Bellemont. From this point on, she would be a fugitive again, hungry, hurting, alone. Was freedom worth it? Now was the time to go back. It was not too late to retrace her steps: she could slip back into her soft cot and nobody would be the wiser.

Nobody except me, she chided herself. Somehow that was worse than hunger or hurt, or being alone. She unwrapped the shoes from her blanket and sat on the moist ground to put them on.

In fact, she was not alone even as she bent over the buckles. Arms encircled her from behind and hands covered her mouth. "Don't make noise," a voice rasped in her ear.

Boy jerked and grunted, trying to break away. She glimpsed baggy-trousered legs.

"It's all right, Boy."

She recognized that raspy voice. "Lookup," she breathed.

"That's right; Lookup here." The woman chuckled and released her. She said briskly, "Let's get going. No telling how soon they find out you gone and set the dogs after you. Might be hunting for me, too."

"Why would they be hunting for you? Nobody knows you're at Bellemont, except down in the quarter, and they wouldn't snitch on you."

To this Lookup made no answer and Boy repeated, "Our people wouldn't tell, would they?"

Slowly she responded. "Not exactly on purpose, maybe. But sorry folks comes in all colors, and some of them just naturally hold it against you that they scared to run and you ain't."

Boy thought of the fellow who had objected when Lookup had preached freedom. She thought of Harriet's loyalty to the Yanceys. The face of Gump, the crosseyed boy, drifted across her mind.

"Hurry long, now," said Lookup. "Talk after." So they ran.

Running was easier with Lookup. Lookup was an expert. She helped Boy bind her pants legs so that they didn't flap and catch on twigs. She showed her how to cover her shoulders and head with her blanket, to let unseen branches and briars scrape cloth rather than flesh. She taught her to trot hunched over, intent on the path, and to alternate running with periods of walking.

Twice they forded shallow streams, and when they came to a deeper creek, she led them downstream to a bridge on the road where they could cross. After that they followed the high road. It seemed to Boy that the sky grew lighter and the road brighter as they ran, but Lookup said she was just getting her night eyes.

They ran until neither of them could run any farther. Then they trudged along until they came to another bridge, where they stopped to drink. They rested under the bridge and ate part of an ashcake that Lookup pulled from her pants pocket. It was still in its charred cabbage-leaf wrapper, warm from her body, and Boy, who only yesterday scorned the slave victuals, ate hungrily.

Lookup said she was going to look for her husband in Freetown.

"I'm headed there too," Boy said, "for Isenhour's."

"You got kin there that can help you?"

Boy tried to think how to answer that. "I was born there," she said at last.

They talked about Bellemont. "What will happen to LeMont and Delilah?" Boy asked her friend.

"They'll run. Not for a while, maybe, but when they have to, they'll run."

"How do you know that? Did LeMont say so?"

"No, it's just a thing you get to where you know. LeMont, he got him a nice spot in the blacksmith shop that he don't want to leave, but when the time come, he'll run. Like you and me. Oh, they's lots of us running."

Boy thought of the columns of runaway ads she had seen in the Freetown newspaper that night so long ago. She remembered the broadsides covering the whole storefront at Feimster's Crossroads. Though the night was growing chilly, she felt suddenly warm and content. "Lots of us." She was in good company. She wanted to roll up in her blanket right here under the bridge and go to sleep, but she knew she couldn't. "Let's get going," she said.

The plan was for them to follow the roads by night, when the dark was their ally, and to sleep through the daytime hours. After false dawn, when light strengthened in the sky ahead of them, they left the road and clambered up a steep bank overgrown with scrub pine. Lookup pushed through the dense vegetation; they crossed a hump of bald rock and dropped down to a tablelike projection that overlooked a tobacco field.

Below the table rock a hollowed-out shelter lay concealed by a tangle of muscadine and trumpet creeper. Lookup drew aside a leafy curtain and motioned Boy to enter the tiny cave. It was not high enough for them to stand upright in, but here they could sleep and rest. She divided the meager remnant of ashcake, and again they ate. From the field they heard the sound of singing: field hands coming out at daybreak to begin the day's work.

"How did you know this place was here?" Boy whispered.

Her companion waved toward the tobacco field. "They told me. Before."

"Before when?"

But Lookup covered her head with her quilt, and Boy after a moment followed her example.

When she woke, the sun was overhead and Lookup was gone. She could scarcely blame her, she thought disconsolately. Traveling alone, the woman could move faster, and more important, need not share her precious provisions.

Just the thought of provisions made Boy hungry. She began rather forlornly to plan what she might look for to eat on her own. Nuts and berries, she supposed. Indians lived off things they found growing in the woods. Squirrels fed on acorns, so they must be edible.

She peeped through a frame of trumpet clusters at the field hands far below. They milled around buckets set on the ground there in the middle of the field. Some children played tag around a wagon. A woman up in the wagon bed nursed a baby. Dinnertime! The field gang was eating dinner. Boy's stomach contracted. To one side of her the orange clusters trembled; the vines shook.

Climbing carefully, Lookup pulled herself with one hand into the cave. In her other hand she carried a gourd filled with Crowder peas. "Dinnertime," she announced with a smile.

Boy looked from the gourd out to the field and back.

"Black driver," her companion explained gleefully, and looking again, Boy identified the slave foreman standing apart from the others.

They ate with their fingers. The peas were hot and delicious. Boy could have eaten the whole gourdful by herself. She daydreamed about an enchanted gourd that kept filling itself up again, no matter how much they ate out of it.

"Lookup," she said wistfully, "do you believe in magic?"

"No indeed, child! Lookup is a good Christian believer. You heard me preaching! You ought to know from that I don't set company with no magic."

"Well, you tell all those stories about magic like you believe them."

"Oh, stories. Them's just stories I got from my Muh.

Muh was full of old tricks and conjures she brung from over the water. What she could really do, though, she could blow fire! If you burnt yourself someways, why she would blow on the place and it wouldn't hurt no more, and you wouldn't get the first beginning of a blister. She done that for me many a time when I burnt myself, and it worked, too."

"Then you do believe in magic," Boy pointed out.

"No ma'am, no ma'am, just the healing, somewhatly, and like that." But Lookup went on to admit she didn't like to hear a scrinch owl holler, for it meant somebody was going to die; and she would never walk near the graveyard at night when the spirits were rising.

Boy snickered. "You don't call that superstition?"

"I call it human nature." Lookup was offended. "Don't tell me you'd sashay over a dead man's grave any time you took a mind to."

"It wouldn't bother me one bit," said Boy. She felt confident that Lookup would never put her to the test.

"And you never kept a lucky piece in your pocket? Like maybe a rabbit's foot?"

"Never." It was true about the rabbit's foot. She didn't intend to talk about the conjure bird; it was too complicated. "Does your mother call herself a Christian too?"

Lookup sighed. "Honey, my Muh come from over the water with her own religion, and her took it back with her."

Her mother was a blue-gummed African, Lookup said, with the marks of her country tattooed on her face, and she talked that queer Afrikee talk, all her life. Vowed she would go back over the water, even though she had lived in this country since she was a girl, and married three times, and had so many younguns you couldn't stir them with a stick. When she grew old and wandering in her mind, she wrapped all her magic charms in a croaker sack one day and walked into the horse pond and drowned.

"They wouldn't bury her in a Christian graveyard," said Lookup bitterly. "Said she were a witch. Muh was as good a woman as ever walked this earth. But it don't matter. Muh believed what she believed, and her faith took her where she wanted to be. Mine will too, when the time come." Her voice trailed off and her eyes grew hazy, as though she looked for something far in the distance, or far within herself.

She said presently, in a normal tone, "You never saw such a nasty mess of roots and chicken eyes and dried blood and batskins and skulls of toads as Muh kept. They was scared to touch any of it when they pulled her out of the water, and they took and thowed all that conjure stuff back in the horse pond."

"Was there a conjure bird in it, do you remember?"

"I don't member none. What you want to know for?" She looked at Boy sharply.

"Just curious."

She was a clever woman, was Lookup. In the waking, waiting hours of afternoon and the many afternoons that followed, she taught Boy how to weave a basket out of honeysuckle vine stripped of its leaves. She showed her where to trim a locust thorn below the angle at the twig to make a beautiful little fishhook. She told her how to trap rabbits in the hollow logs they called gums, and how you could catch possums at night in a cornfield. She showed her the spark that flew from flint chips when she struck them together, and that would start a fire, she said, if the spark fell on punkwood.

Lookup could teach you everything, Boy discovered, but she didn't really know anything. Of all the days in the week, Lookup knew only the name of Sunday. If it wasn't Sunday, it was a work day. She was also ignorant of the months and understood the year only by its seasons. She did not know how old she was; she had been told she was born "in hoe time"; her mother left off chopping cotton in order to give birth, and the day after, returned to the field and took up her hoe again.

Lookup could tell fantastic stories about everything she had ever seen. She was a grown girl, she said, the year the stars fell, and she described how fiery shooting stars crossed and recrossed the night sky, and how everybody thought the world was coming to an end, and they ran out to the brush harbor and prayed for forgiveness before they all should die. But the next day was a work day same as always, and the world went on same as always, and that was many long years ago, said Lookup.

When night fell and they set out, Lookup the storyteller was silenced. They needed all their energy for traveling, but more important, they dared not let the night patrol hear them. In July's hot weather, horsemen were out on the roads every night. Boy and Lookup would hear hoof-beats in the distance and leap for concealment. From woods and ditches they watched the men gallop past, always in pairs, searching, chasing, intent.

The sight of them sweeping past terrified Boy. The law allowed those men to whip any slave they caught, and some enjoyed whipping as they would a sport. Harriet had seen the patrol whip her own father in South Carolina; they made everybody watch, she said, to teach them a lesson.

"They don't scare me," Lookup said. "Down off of them big old horses, they ain't nothen but little white men."

Nevertheless, they took no risks. The strain of their fugitive existence had begun to tell on them.

– 16 –

THE MAGIC BALLPOINT PEN

Humid weather during the dog days wore them down and often made their waiting hours too hot for sleeping. Through the oppressive afternoons, Boy wished for cool night, for relief and for the hours of running that brought them closer to Freetown. Yet as they neared their goal, her anxiety increased, and for the first time since Bellemont, she began to have doubts.

"Don't worry about it," Lookup told her. "We're going to find your people."

"My people," Boy mused, and to herself she added, My mother, Overtha's mother. Will I love her? She wondered.

They had sheltered that morning in the cellar of a burnt-out cabin at the edge of a field, and they had nothing to eat, though they were able to drink from a stagnant pool at the lower end of the dugout. Through the morning they had dozed and dreamed of food. "Suppose that's not my mother at Isenhour's?" Boy said to Lookup. "I'm scared to find out, now that we're almost there."

"Don't be scared. Have faith."

Easy to say, Boy argued despondently. She couldn't pretend to have faith. She wasn't a strong Christian like Lookup.

"I ain't talking that kind of faith, that you wait around for what you want to happen," Lookup said. "You got to make it happen. Like my Muh done, when she went back over the water."

"What about those people who claimed she was a witch and drowned herself, so they wouldn't let her be buried in a Christian graveyard?"

"What about them?" said Lookup strongly. "Muh done what she believed in. She weren't one to set around till she died of the old sets." She admired her mother, that old African who resolved to return over the water, and who at last did, in her own way. Lookup too would do what she believed in. She was confident of finding her husband, in Freetown or wherever he might be. She was going to make that happen.

A wonderful sense of purpose surged through Boy. She forgot the heat and her discomfort; she forgot that she was hungry. Lookup was right. She must stop wishing for magic; instead she must make the magic happen. At least she could change things.

Lately she had whiled away the afternoons playing teacher to Lookup, who was learning her ABC's. There would be no more play school, Boy resolved. From now on, studies were going to begin in earnest for her pupil. In the sweltering, burnt-out cabin, on the dirt floor, she began scratching combinations of letters and words for the first reading lesson. Through the sultry afternoon they pored together over the work, Lookup groaning with un-accustomed effort, Boy urging her on. Before they knew it, dusk was upon them, and they climbed cautiously out of their cellar into a field of tasseling corn.

The road took them that night past the store at Feimster's Crossroads, where Boy crept onto the porch and ripped down an armload of the broadsides posted there.

"You a fool!" Lookup scolded her. "What if the dogs got after you?"

"But they didn't! And now we've got some real paper for you to write on, and real print for your reading lessons."

"You could've got caught. They could've caught you and me too."

Boy said arrogantly, "No, they couldn't. We're smarter than they are. Anyway, it's done now. Beats dying of the old sets, doesn't it?"

In the days that followed, Lookup's schooling intensified. On her own, she began to pick out phrases in the stolen broadsides. She struggled to make sense of sentences. She progressed. With much coaching from Boy, she read aloud haltingly one day:

$25 REWARD

Ranaway or stolen before Christmas, a Negro girl OVERTHA, from James Yancey, Esq. of Bellemont community. She is about 12 yrs of age, small in size, not having achieved her growth, bold in manner, looks you in the face when spoken to. She has all her teeth and a Y brand on the cheek, but no mark of the lash. Her mother belongs to Mr. Isenhour in Freetown, and she may be lurking in that neighborhood. The above reward will be paid for proof to convict any white person of taking her away or harboring her; or $10 for her apprehension and delivery in some safe jail, where the undersigned can get her.

James Yancey, Esq.

Boy asked keenly, "Do you understand what you've read?"

Lookup hung her head. "I don't know what none of them big words means."

Boy started to say, Well, Overtha means *me.* That's me, Boy, in that poster. It would be a relief just to have somebody know about her. She wished she could tell her friend, but something prevented her. After all, she didn't know Lookup's real name either.

Writing came much easier for Lookup. Her nimble fingers quickly took to copying out the lessons Boy set her. The simple tales of Black John and Old Raw Head and Bloody Bones accumulated on the backs of auction notices, and the storyteller read them aloud to her teacher. She rewrote and read aloud again, over and over, enchanted with the sound of her own words, in love with the magic ballpoint pen.

"It's nothing but a cheap plastic pen," said Boy.

Lookup knew better. Any slave knew better. There were masters who would cut off the finger of a slave caught with pen and paper, "Cause, see, they might write they own pass—"

In midsentence, Lookup turned slowly. Boy's mouth opened. With one incredulous voice they repeated the words, *"Write our own pass!"* and they fell into each other's arms.

"I don't believe this. I simply don't believe we didn't think of this before," Boy kept saying.

Lookup was trembling so violently that she could do nothing except admire. She hung over Boy's shoulder and watched her shear lovely blank margins off a broadside with a blade of sawgrass.

"Praise the Lord, us don't have to worry about patterrollers no more, no more!"

Boy said, "Not as much, anyway. We're going to have written permission in our pockets to go wherever we go. Hand me the pen—and quit leaning on me! I'm nervous enough without you shaking me too."

Lookup clasped her hands prayerfully and stood aside.

"All right now. 'Lookup has leave to pass and repass—' "

" 'Lucie,' " said Lookup. "Write it 'Lucie.' "

Boy said, "Oh. Is Lucie your real name?"

"Yes," said the woman, and with a sly, bright glance, "What's *your* real name?"

"They've always just called me Boy."

"You ain't maybe a *girl* called Boy? Maybe a girl name of Overtha?"

Instinctively Boy prepared to bluster a denial, but Lookup's twinkle stopped her. "How did you find out?" she asked, deflated.

"I knowed all along," Lookup said airily. "All of us knowed. They ain't no secrets in the quarter."

"I bet Harriet told you. She knew."

"Harriet didn't have to tell nobody. They all knowed. Honey, little LeMont and little Overtha, they was hatched in the quarter. You think they'd forget which one was which?"

"I still can't believe Mrs. Yancey would go along with a gag like that."

"Oh, white folks," Lookup sniffed. "Sure you fooled the white folks. They don't pay no tention. We all look alike to them, didn't you never hear 'em say that? They don't see us and they don't hear us. A lady like Miz Yancey is nice and kind, but she ask you a question, you know what the answer is, don't you?"

"Yes'm," said Boy. "Yes'm, yes'm and yes'm. Any more questions?"

"Yes'm," said Lookup. "Where this magic pen come from?"

She felt so tempted! But would even this storyteller swallow Boy's story? Would she believe automobiles and telephones? Radios and computers and rockets to the moon? Ice cream? It was simpler just to tell part of the truth. "My mother gave it to me," she said.

All unexpectedly her voice broke. It was mentioning Mama that did it. She should have known better. She dropped her head and stared at the buckles slowly blurring on her shoes.

Lookup said, "Oh, honey. I didn't go to make you cry. Don't, honey, Lookup'll get you to Isenhour's." She pulled Boy into the circle of her arms.

"Maybe that's not my mother at Isenhour's," Boy wailed. It hurt so much, it helped so much, for Lookup to hold her.

"Sh-hh, sh-hh. You got to have faith." For a long time Lookup soothed and rocked her and murmured the age-old sounds of a mother consoling her child. "You know you going to find you mammy."

My mammy, Boy brooded. Will I love her?

Thoughts of eating obsessed them, and for good reason, for some days they found no food at all. They always searched along the edges of ponds and streams, hoping to find a wild duck's nest. The eggs had to be eaten raw; Lookup knew how to make a fire using her flintrock chips, but they dared not let a thread of smoke betray them.

When they reached the vicinity of Linney's Mill, Boy remembered the pyramid of meal that sifted down from a chute onto the platform. For two days thereafter, they feasted on cakes made of meal mixed with water and dried on a rock in the sun while they slept.

For the most part, they lived off the generosity of slaves along the way, who willingly shared their allotments, though these were often scanty. Many a slave consumed his peck of meal and pint of molasses early in the week and wound up with little or nothing to divide.

They fared best on the large breeding farms, where extra food was issued for growing children. On these farms the masters appreciated the value of what they were raising for sale: robust slaves brought in more cash than a bumper field crop.

Cedar Springs, where they arrived on a rainy Saturday morning, was just such a breeding farm. They settled in for a weekend at the children's house, to eat and to dry out their soaked shoes and clothing. Lookup gathered the children around her to entertain them with stories about a wily slave named Pompey, while Boy sat down by a pile of seeded cotton lint and began carding it for the spinner. By helping out at simple tasks, she tried to show her gratitude toward the various cabin mammies who had sheltered her and Lookup in their long journey through the North Carolina mountains. Today the work soothed her jittery nerves as well.

Last night, in between squally bouts of rain, they had heard the screech owl cry. Its ghostly, shuddering wail followed them all along the road to Cedar Springs.

"Somebody die, for sure," said Lookup.

"Is it following us, do you think?"

"Following somebody."

Boy didn't want to believe that, but she learned she had to, somewhatly, as Lookup was fond of saying. An aged manslave had just died at Cedar Springs, the doctor-granny there informed them. Granny was a tall, bright-skinned woman, who, besides supervising the children, did the cooking, concocted herb remedies, dosed the sick and presided over the plantation's births and deaths. Today, in this room, it would be her duty to wash and shroud the mortal remains of Uncle Jubah.

"Maybe best you not tarry here over Sunday," she warned Boy, looking worried. There were already two runaways hiding out down at the carpenter's shop, and extra patrols were being brought in from the next district to help round them up. She rotated Boy's shoes at the fireplace. "The rain letting up, and you shoes most dry."

Boy turned to consult with her friend, but Lookup was already deep in her story. "It was Pompey's job to shine Master's boots for church," she was saying. The youngsters around her giggled their anticipation. "One Saturday night, Pompey put them boots on hisself to go dancing in, and my, didn't he look handsome, dancing all night in Master's boots! But when it come time to shine 'em up and set 'em by Master's door, Pompey's feets so swole up, the boots wouldn't come off—"

The cabin door opened and a crosseyed boy brought in a long garment draped over one arm. Boy averted her face and bent low, as if to her work. She had hoped, by staying in the children's house at Cedar Springs, to avoid meeting Gump again. Now here he was. She dared not look him in the face. With dread she heard him say, "Oh, Granny, those be fair buckle-shoes. Who them pretty shoes belong to?"

"Belong to Old Raw Head and Bloody Bones, that's who to. Get on out of here, fore I lay you on the cooling board stead of Uncle."

Gump took his time inspecting the shoes on the hearth. He departed only after he made a slow detour, humming all the while, around Boy and her pile of cotton lint. She hoped he didn't see her shiver.

– 17 –

A SAGA OF SHOES

"We've got to get out of here," Boy told Lookup as soon as she could speak to her privately. "Gump set the overseer onto a couple of fellows and me back at Christmastime, and that's how I got caught. Oh, he's a traitor! If he snitched once, you know he'll do it again."

Lookup hurried out to see what she could learn from the carriage boy about the patrols. Granny wrapped salt pork in a cabbage leaf for Boy and helped her fill her pocket with meal. The rain had stopped, but the air lay thick and damp outside, and inside, fireplace heat made the room oppressive.

Two men carried the cooling board into the cabin, and two others a sheeted form, which they placed on the high, narrow table.

> *In this life of heavy load,*
> *Lord, spare the weary traveler*
> *Along the heavenly road.*

Granny sang mournfully as she prepared the body for burial. The toddlers huddled together in a corner. Boy

149

kept her distance, too. She had never seen a dead person, and it made her feel spooky, being under the same roof with Uncle Jubah. She wished Lookup would come back so they could leave.

The day drew to a close and the heavy sky darkened in the west, spreading its pall over the mountains. Boy peeped nervously out at the road that ran through the quarter, willing Lookup to return. She saw Gump come out of the cabin across the road and join three men bearing a long, soot-smudged box on their shoulders. It was Uncle Jubah's coffin. She remained at the window as they carried it into the room and tried to stop her ears to the sounds of shifting, shuffling, grunting, tried not to think of the body being lifted into that sinister case. Oh, why didn't Lookup come?

Suddenly she saw Gump race back across the road, doubled over, carrying something close against his body. He ran into the cabin opposite the children's house. Sneaky! She thought of the pink cake, so long ago, how Gump had sneaked her portion for himself and mocked her with it. Sneaky? He was just plain sorry.

Gump walked out of the cabin emptyhanded, head up, glaring all about. He strolled off down the road, swinging his arms and whistling, the way a sneak thief would. But what would he have stolen from this poor cabin, from the very room where Uncle Jubah lay in his coffin?

Shoes, of course! Her good buckled shoes sitting openly on the hearth. She whirled to look, but she knew without looking: the square-toed shoes were gone.

The rude smell of sage filled the room. The cooling board had been removed, and an open coffin replaced it on the trestles. Boy took one brief, unwilling look.

A grizzled old man lay inside, arms crossed high and narrow on his chest, as though avoiding the walls of his enclosure. Now mourners began a slow procession through the door and around the coffin to pay their last respects to Uncle Jubah. Granny stood by, clasping a bunch of silvery leaves to her breast. Boy approached her timidly to whisper of her loss.

"There your shoes is, right by the fire," Granny pointed. "Ho! Where them shoes gone to? They was here when Gump brought me the funeral herbs." She stooped and laid a branch of the silver leaves on the fireplace coals. The aroma of sage strengthened.

"Do you think anybody . . . could have moved them someplace else?"

Granny switched her palm in exasperation. "Gump. Gump'd steal the coffin lid off of Uncle Jubah if us didn't nail it down." She patted Boy's arm. "Don't worry, son. I grannied that Gump from the day he's born, and he knows to mind me. I'll get your shoes back for you."

But when? Boy felt reluctant to ask her, with poor Uncle Jubah lying there. She must simply go and get the shoes for herself.

Outside, moist air enfolded her. The woods and fields had dissolved in estuaries of fog that flowed in from the west. Already the farthest cabins of the quarter appeared afloat where a tidal vapor washed the road. Her spirits lifted. She had come to love fog—the runaway's friend.

The door of the cabin across the road stood slightly ajar, and she slid inside without knocking. It was an ordinary slave cabin, like the others she had been in during their journey; she knew it by heart—the drab, dim interior, the one shuttered window, the bunk pegged to the wall. This cabin had a loose plank floor, or part of a plank floor, someone's after-hours project. Three rough boards leaned against the wall in a corner. She ran her hands over the bunk, stirred through a pile of rags and lifted each loose plank to peer underneath. There was really no place to hide anything in a slave cabin.

She gave a final look around. A noise outside the door sent her scurrying behind the boards in the corner, and she almost lost her balance as she trod on some tomatoes stored there.

Hark from the tomb a doleful sound–

It was Gump's voice, and he was singing! To each phrase of the funeral hymn, he added a jaunty drum roll with his bone clickers.

My ears hear a tender cry. (rattat tatta tat-tat)

He stepped inside the cabin door and kicked it shut, singing all the while.

> *A living man come through the ground*
> *Where we may shortly lie. (rattat tatta tat-tat)*

Panicky, she tried to think what to do. Then, between the cracks of her hiding place, she saw that he was wearing her square-toed shoes. Dancing in *her* shoes, the while he jazzed up the hymn with his bone clickers.

> *Here in this clay may be your bed,*
> *In spite of all your toil—*

Her clenched fist felt the lump in her pocket. Meal, salt pork—ha! She'd teach Gump! She unwrapped the greasy chunk and began rubbing it over her face and arms.

Let all the wise bow reverent head
Must lie as low as ours. (rattat tatta tat-tat)

"Raw Head and Bloody Bones . . ." A ghostly drone halted Gump's concert.

"Whuh. . . ?"

A frightful face floated out at him, a chalky face with blood oozing into its deep, staring eyes. Clutching hands reached for him, fingers dripped blood on him and he staggered backward.

"Oo-oo-ooo . . . Raw Head and Bloody Bones come to get you."

He shrieked. He fell. He scrambled for the door, regained his feet, and screaming for mercy, tore up the road toward the big house.

Boy stood in the road and watched him run. Giggling, she wiped meal from her face and cleaned the squashed tomatoes from her hands and hair. It was almost worth losing her shoes.

"Hide, quick! Patterrollers!" It was Lookup at her side.

Together they dropped to the ground. They managed to crawl on their bellies between two cabins just as a group of horsemen cantered down to where Boy had been standing.

The patrols spread out along the quarter in pairs, one rider of each pair holding the horses while the other dismounted and searched the cabins. Not twenty feet from where Boy lay, a man on horseback seemed to stare directly into her eyes. But the restless horse stamped and turned, and with that, the man looked away. Instantly Boy and Lookup slithered toward the upland meadow that lay in back of the quarter.

For a long time they crawled on hands and knees in the wet grass. Presently a band of fog obscured the line of cabins and they stood up and ran, feeling horribly visible in the open meadow. They crossed a hummocky knoll and reached woods on the hilltop before they dared to stop. There they looked down over a cliff of fog; beyond it, cabin roofs could be seen and moving forms along the quarter road. They pushed their way into thick underbrush and tumbled to the ground, exhausted.

"Gump stole my shoes," Boy said bitterly, when at last she could speak.

Lookup said, "Well, I ain't going back to get 'em for you!" It was lucky they got away when they did, she said. Saturday-night passes had been canceled for miles around. That meant a thorough search. But they would wait it out up here in the woods. In a couple of days maybe they could take to the roads again.

Boy said, "Gump will snitch on us, I can promise you that."

"Who going to listen to Gump?"

Still, a silence fell between them, and Boy sensed that Lookup wasn't as confident as she sounded.

They talked, inevitably, of food. Boy sucked her fingers for the flavor of tomato that lingered there. "I still have a little meal in my pocket." They divided her small store, licking their palms slowly to make it last. She produced the salt pork also, but stowed it away again because it would make them want water. Thirst would drive them from hiding quicker than hunger. Just thinking about it made her thirsty.

"Do you hear something?" Lookup lifted one hand. Stillness and fog lay all around.

"No—yes. Like a kind of humming?"

"Yes."

The sound crept toward them. They strained, listening, and looking into the dense cloud that veiled the slope below.

"I thought I saw—"

"—fog, rasseling round down there."

It shifted as they watched, shreds of vapor rising, settling, spreading out. Then a twinkle, immediately blotted out.

"There! Did you see that?" Boy asked.

"Yes."

The humming intensified. The fog brightened, and Boy glimpsed a second twinkle, then another. "Oh, Lookup."

"Sh-h-h."

The humming took shape, the fog glowed and the glow advanced in their direction. From the humming there emerged a song.

> *Going to carry this body to the graveyard,*
> *Graveyard, don't you know me?*
> *Going to carry this body to the graveyard,*
> *To lay this body down.*

A line of wavering lights broke free of the glowing fog.

" 'Lay this body down,' " Lookup quoted solemnly. "They bringing the old fellow to bury."

"To bury where? Is there a graveyard up here?"

"Must be where we ran over them chuckholes."

That hummocky knoll—that was the slave cemetery. Without realizing, Boy had tramped on one sunken grave after another. She shuddered.

Torches burned through the fog, and now the procession was clearly seen mounting the knoll. Flaring lightwood knots disclosed the rupture of a newly dug grave. Uncle Jubah's coffin moved slowly forward.

With poles and ropes, men lowered the narrow box while the crowd watched. Someone said a prayer. Granny reminded the Almighty of Uncle Jubah's blameless life. A man sobbed, and a slow march around the gravesite began. Once, twice, the mourners circled, and completing the third round, they stooped for handfuls of clay and tossed them down onto the coffin. At last, men with shovels filled in the grave and dragged forward a peaked, rooflike structure to set in place over the mounded dirt.

"What's that?" Boy whispered. The mourners began departing, much faster than they had approached, for a light drizzle had begun and the torches were sputtering.

"Grave lid. Cover up the dirt till it set, so rain don't wash away the corpse." Lookup shifted uneasily and suggested, "Maybe us go in the woods back a piece from here."

She was scared of graveyards, Boy remembered. But the drizzle was steady now and might easily work up to a soaker. "Let's get under that little roof out of the rain," Boy proposed.

"Under a grave lid?" Lookup was horrified. "Right on top of a corpse?"

"Then let's haul the roof up here."

"Too heavy, too heavy." Lookup was anxious to leave.

"I bet it's not all that heavy. You're strong and so am I, and we don't have to carry it. We could probably drag it up here easy. It'd be a good, dry place to sleep," she tempted.

Little by little Boy persuaded her. But, "Get outta my way, if they come any ghosts," Lookup advised. "I be cutting a road thu the woods, running."

Silently they crept down to the graveyard and positioned themselves at one end of the shelter. Each took a corner. At the signal they would pull together. Boy looked across confidently and mouthed, *Now.*

Before they could move it, the roof moved itself, right up out of their hands, and two tall figures leaped out at them.

"Ghosts!" Lookup squeaked.

Boy shot up the hill and crashed into the woods. Something tripped her and she fell. She fought to get up, but vicious briars bound her to the ground. To her astonishment, she heard Lookup calling, calling tenderly.

"Ike, don't run! It's Lucie." And in that same warm, loving tone she said, "Come back, Isaac. It's your Muh, honey; wait for Muh."

"Lucie!"

"Muh. Oh, Muh." That was Isaac speaking—Boy's lost friend Isaac. She tore herself free from the vine and parted the bushes.

- 18 -

THE CONNECTION

Muh.

"My Muh, she were a storyteller," Isaac had boasted at the Christmas party. Boy might have made the connection back when the children at Bellemont begged for a story, another story from the storyteller.

I never make the right connection, she thought dismally, looking on at the little family reunion in which she played no part. At the edge of the graveyard the three of them rocked, locked together, and they could not stop repeating one another's names. Boy felt left out, and sad, and homesick.

Then Lookup remembered her. "Boy?" she called, with a lilt. "Come out. It's all right; these my folks." She ran to her and drew her out of hiding. "My partner," she explained to her family.

"Boy!" Isaac yelled. He grabbed her and hugged her, danced her around, held her tight and—yes, wept for joy! "Oh, Pa, it's Boy, our Boy! He got away, he come back, he did!"

Ike and Lookup stood close together. The mother chuckled. "You sure right, son. Boy come back, but you wrong about *he*. This Boy is a *she*."

Isaac did not exactly shove Boy away, but he did stop hugging her. "She?" he accused her. "You a girl?" And he accused Lookup also, "You telling one of your stories, Muh. Boy ain't no girl!"

Lookup merely smiled.

For a while Isaac stalked about angrily. When Ike and Lookup turned away together, he muttered to Boy, "You didn't really fool me."

"I never tried to," she said. "Boy is just what people call me. I said so in the beginning."

And at last he said handsomely, "I wish all along that you be safe, and that we find you again some day."

What a reunion it was! They dragged the grave lid up to the woods, and inside its shelter they celebrated. The men brought out cornshuck packages of hoecake and kush, and they ate. Late into the night they talked, filling in the pieces of their lives that had dropped out of the puzzle. They rejoiced over the rifle shot that had missed its mark and marveled at how Uncle Jubah's funeral had brought them together.

Ike described how they hid in two coffins in the carpenter shop until they could be smuggled out as pallbearers marching to the graveyard. A melancholy rain rattled the rough thatching over their heads, but neither it nor the leaky funeral roof could dilute their spirits. Rain, like the fog, was a friend and protector, the grave lid a fortress. In their kinship they knew themselves to be invincible.

Ike was jubilant with plans for the future. He had learned a lot in the lonely fugitive months. Together they could head for free territory—Ohio, and then Canada, he said; and he had heard of a whole town of free blacks living in Virginia, near Richmond. So many exciting possibilities to choose from! They had never had a choice in the past.

"But first we have to go to Freetown," said Lookup.

Ike said, puzzled, "Freetown? What we need to go there for?"

"You don't need to," Boy said. "I can manage by myself."

Isaac protested, with a worried squint at his father, "We ought to get her back to her folks, Pa."

He needn't have worried. Ike said immediately, "Course we will."

"No, really—"

"We will," said Lookup firmly.

Freetown wasn't all that far from where they were. "One more night on the road and we have you back in your mammy's arms," Ike promised. "You almost home."

Boy's long journey was nearly over. Almost "home." Late that night she lay awake and thought of the mammy she would meet at last. Mama and Daddy were on her mind, too. She felt obscurely disloyal to them, but she didn't mean to be. She just needed so much to belong somewhere. Boy sighed and twisted on her bed of leaves and listened to the rain on the roof.

Before dawn the next morning, they moved the grave lid back to its proper place and crossed under clearing skies to the other side of the hill. One by one they scuttled past the lofty knob at its peak, but Boy paused there to look at the valley, and what she saw clutched at her heart. In the distance, a familiar lake, interrupted along its length by trees, flashed silvery signals. Bellemont!

Boy felt faint. Bellemont, *there*? Now? Something crazy must be going on. She had left Bellemont weeks ago, she

was close to Freetown, almost home. Ike had said so yesterday. Could they have traveled in a circle? She wouldn't
let herself breathe, holding in her wits. She knew Bellemont Overlook too well to be mistaken about it—the bluff,
the winding staircase of boulders leading to the granite
knob. Along the valley, Yancey country lay placid in the
summer sunlight.

Boy looked in vain for the mill at the neck of the valley
where the river entered, for the mansion on the hill above
the lake. It was not trees that hid them from her view.
They simply weren't there any more. They had been gone
for years; the Park Service tore them all down when it
acquired the land. She remembered Daddy telling her
that. Daddy . . .

The valley darkened subtly as she gazed upon it, as
though a cloud had stealthily smothered the sun. Yet she
looked up to a sky of perfect blue, blank of any cloud
except for the vapor trail of a jet so high above she could
neither see the airplane nor hear its flight.

An airplane in 1854, she thought dazedly. Would
Lookup believe an airplane if she saw it? Do *I* believe it?
Then she thought with a jolt, Of course I believe it—and if
I believe it—

"Boy! Git down from there!" That was Ike, ordering her
off the exposed overlook.

She rushed to him. Ike wouldn't deceive her. "That
looks like Bellemont Lake to me, Ike. Down there. Do you
see the lake?"

He looked where she pointed. "You must got the head
misery, Boy. Ain't no lake out there."

He grabbed her wrist and yanked her to the bluff she
recognized, from whose overhang the huge tree had

tipped and fallen in some wet season. Its upended roots spread a sod roof over the rim of the bluff, and honeysuckle tangled the lattice of its branches. Below a bank studded with mica and soapstone ran a shallow stream.

"Here's where I crossed! This is where—"

"Never mind where. Climb down behind them vines."

Ike released her to lead the way down a ladder of branches, and at the bottom he plunged behind a wall of honeysuckle.

Boy followed him reluctantly. She really needed time to think. She felt dizzy and off-balance, and not just from her shaky descent on the branches. Across the shallows below, a sandy shoal shimmered in the noonday sun. The light so dazzled her she had to look away from it, but not before she saw (or wished she saw?) her sneakers parked on the shore, right where she had left them.

"Come inside, Boy!" Isaac urged her from behind the vines.

She ducked into their hideout, but she still felt disoriented from what she had seen; and she immediately parted the vines to look again. From that sandy shoal, a peculiar power pulled her gaze. She felt suffused and surrounded by its aura; the very shimmering seemed to be drawing her to it, and she experienced a strange sensation of teetering on an awesome brink.

"Oh, conjure bird," she implored, as she had so many times before. But something clicked in her mind, and at that moment she realized that she was not so much talking to the talisman as she was to herself.

"This is a good place," Ike was saying, as from a great distance. "We got water. . . ."

Whatever magic the conjure bird might or might not

have, Boy possessed her own powers. She was free to choose, and she understood that now. Whether it had been her free choice or some unconscious wish to believe in the conjure bird that took her into the world of her ancestors she could not quite figure out, and perhaps never would. It did not matter. Her powers might lead her to act foolishly again—her actions certainly had brought her a peck of trouble up to now—but the choice was hers. She could choose to cross the water once again, to claim her own world.

The shimmering over there subsided. The brilliant noonday light no longer blinded her. She could stare at her sneakers without discomfort. Her grubby sneakers resting on the sand emanated no power, no aura— emanated nothing, in fact, beyond their own sneakerdom. Still it was the sight of them that jogged her—she could go home. She could go home!

Behind her, Ike murmured on. "Downstream, tonight, Freetown . . ."

Boy whirled. "No, Ike. Not to Freetown. I've changed my mind. I'm going across the water instead. Come with me."

He drew back, his kind face wrinkling with distress. She longed to reassure him, though she knew she must speak cautiously. "Come with me. You'll be safe. We'll all be safe. There isn't any slavery where I'm going to take you."

It wasn't that he mistrusted her, she could tell, but his eyes grew mournful. "It's what I have to do," she tried to explain. "It's like when you and Isaac ran away to find Lookup."

He answered her, but what he said sounded faint and

only vaguely familiar, like the echo of a language she could not quite recall.

Isaac came and peered into her face. Isaac would understand, her good friend Isaac.

"You tell him," she begged. "Something's happened— it's like a sign—my sneakers, I mean, over there on the sandbar. Do you see where I'm pointing?" She felt silly talking like that about her sneakers. She gestured and shouted now, "Isaac, can't you hear me?", trying to make him understand.

He bent closer and said something to her, but his words were scarcely more than vibrations that trailed off into a kind of humming. When he straightened, it was as though he too receded, and his father at his shoulder faded and drifted farther still.

She was losing them, she saw, and it made her frantic. She was powerless to coax them into her century, where she had it in her power to help them. She could not touch them; she could not hold them; they retreated beyond her reach, as into an immense and mysterious cavern.

"Lookup," she pleaded, "won't you come with me over the water? It's not my fault; I have to go back. But if you come too, we can all be free. . . ."

Lookup smiled tenderly. Her face grew soft and indistinct.

"Don't go!" Boy entreated. "You belong to me; I need you!"

It struck her cruelly that she had never told Lookup how much she loved her, and now they were parting without her being able to hear it. Lookup, who had given Boy so much, so much.

"Wait!" Boy fumbled in her pocket. "Take my ballpoint pen."

Lookup's fingers were like feathers that brushed hers and floated off palely. In the space before her, the ballpoint pen appeared to be floating too, for a moment, before it vanished.

A cheap ballpoint pen. It was all Boy had to give her, the best she knew to do. But it was enough, because to Lookup the pen was magic, and now the magic of writing could never be taken from her. Perhaps the magic pen would carry Lookup and her family to their freedom.

She was all alone. Looking about her, it was difficult to see how four people had ever crowded into this cramped place against the bluff. She felt trapped in there and breathless. The enclosed atmosphere was humid and stifling. She had to get out.

She ripped the vines from in front of her and splashed into the stream. The cold water shocked her so that she shrieked and halted at the edge, balanced on one leg. North Carolina mountain streams run cold, even in midsummer.

"Come back!" It sounded like Isaac's merry voice, heard from a long way off. She spun around joyfully, but no one was there. The niche against the bluff was vacant and scarcely looked like a niche, with the vines spread apart where she had ripped them, opening the hiding place to the light. Did Isaac really call to her? Was Isaac real? she wondered, half in a daze. Had all that happened, or had she dreamed it happened?

"Come back, Boy!" It wasn't Isaac. It was Junior Jurnigan, standing on the sandspit and calling to her. "Your mother says for you to come back now."

She picked her way through the shallows to where he stood.

"Hey, what happened to your face?" he asked. His voice sounded unnaturally loud.

She bent and picked up her sneakers so as not to look at him. If everything that had happened to her showed in her face—! From inside the one sneaker she drew the bit of soapstone from its hiding place.

That was all it was, a piece of soapstone, crudely carved, nothing sinister about it, not its nubbins of feet, not the gouged-out hollows meant to be its eyes. Still, just holding the carving in her hand stirred a profound response in Boy. Isaac, Lookup, Ike—they belonged to her forever now, just as she belonged to them, because of their connection, because of this talisman.

Junior said, "Oh, your daddy's conjure bird! Can I hold it once? Please?" He turned it from side to side and fingered its outlines. "It really does feel soapy. I wonder how they worked magic with it. Do you believe it? That it was magic, I mean?"

She looked back across the stream. "Somewhatly."

On the trail to camp she asked Junior in her most casual tone, "I wasn't gone too long, was I?"

He said, in that same loud voice, "Who cares, at a picnic? You can throw a hamburger on the grill whenever you get hungry."

But in the picnic area, they were all standing around where the table was set. It was clear they had been waiting for her, and her brother was not as courteous as Junior.

"Who do you think you are, anyway?" he yelled. "We been waiting on you for hours."

Daddy said, "Hours? Now, LeMont. Ten minutes."

Boy thought, Ten minutes! The most important months of my life!

Mama said, "Honey! What did you do to your face? Your cheek is all bloody!"

"I cut it on a broken branch," said Boy. She could feel the blood, still warm and wet on her cheek.

"Don't touch it, dear," said Mrs. Jurnigan. "Your hands aren't clean." Mrs. Jurnigan taught second grade, and she often sounded like a teacher. She peered at Boy's cheek. "It's quite a deep wound. I believe it may need a stitch or two to close it."

It seemed to Boy that they all were talking a lot louder than they needed to. "It doesn't hurt," she mumbled.

Mama said nervously, "Suppose I run her over to the hospital in Morganton."

"That's what I'd do," said Mrs. Jurnigan, "if she were a pupil of mine."

"It doesn't hurt; it'll be all right," Boy said again. She remembered very well how quickly her cheek had healed after Ike doctored it with tobacco juice. She couldn't resist adding, "It just needs some baccy to draw the pizen."

"What?" said Daddy.

"You all go ahead and eat," Boy said. "I'll wash my face and put a Band-Aid on and be right with you." She felt raw and exposed. Their loud, clipped talk confused and bothered her; it was so different from the soft rhythms of the speech she had grown accustomed to. She needed some time by herself.

But no. "Mama will wash it for you," said Mama.

Daddy took a look before they put the Band-Aid on and said the wound was jagged, but not too bad. "You might get a little scar from it, though, an X to mark the spot."

"Not an X," said Boy, "a Y."

"What?" said Daddy.

Then Mama saw all the scratches on her arms and said, "Mercy, child, where on earth did you go to get scratched up like this?"

"Just to the Overlook. The path is overgrown—"

"Up there checking out Yancey country, were you?" Daddy teased. He knew how family traditions bored Boy.

"Yes," she said soberly. "Where our people come from."

Her mother and father exchanged a glance that Boy didn't see. Instead, she saw Yancey country and thought of their people. Her people. Part of her would always yearn for that unknown mother deep in her past. Oh, conjure bird, let Mammy know I love her, she willed, and gently touched the soapstone carving in her pocket. Then she drew it out and extended it to her father.

He stood looking at the carving and said to Boy, "As you grow older, sweetheart, I hope you'll appreciate what this little fellow means to our family."

"I think I already do," said Boy.